Virgin to the Life

John Collins

LET'S RETHINK THAT
ATLANTA, GA
www.letsrethinkthat.com

You may contact John Collins at: johncollins280@gmail.com
Twitter: authorjohncollins
Instagram: princeofpages

Virgin to the Life Copyright © 2014

Dedication

This is dedicated to our LGBT youth: Know that we were not made to simply fit in. We are not supposed to be the status quo. We were born different. We were built different. We are here for divine purpose. Find and use your voice as I have...

Table of Contents

Formal Introductions

In life, we have the daunting task of self-discovery. I was practically on the edge of my seat aboard this airplane eagerly waiting the unfolding of the next chapter of my life anxious about what adulthood would bring my way? As I ripped open the small packet of complimentary dry roasted peanuts, I placed my head back against the headrest and gazed through the window. The slow movement of the clouds passing under the aircraft put me in a peaceful mindset as I looked back over my life thus far. I popped a few salty peanuts into my mouth. My attention then focused on my reflection within the confines of the porthole. I was looking at myself with a different pair of eyes. It's interesting that as an Army brat, I had the privilege of meeting people from all walks of life before I was able to meet myself. Accepting my sexuality was a process. Throughout high school, I felt isolated - "different." I felt as if I was the only boy who liked boys...

Being different led me to the very definition of acceptance at the age of sixteen. Being different brought me closer to God – the one who knew me before I knew myself. One Sunday in church, I sat listening intently to a sermon dealing with prayer. Pastor Joyner told us that we often pray in a repetitious manner mulling over the same issue. And though there is nothing overtly wrong with this, one doesn't allow God to do what He needs to do. We pester Him and

1

dwell on the same issue, which takes away from our faith. I laughed to myself thinking how I was guilty of this. Pastor stated, "You must pray, no doubt but learn how to let go, and let God. Put it in Gods hand and in his timing your prayer will be answered. You won't have to question." I decided to go home that night and pray a prayer that I had been afraid to pray. I was scared of what the answer might be. I was scared to even bring it before God. I felt that the sky was going to crack open with a thunderous voice shouting down at me in anger and disgust declaring, *"HOW DARE YOU!"*

I waited until the family was all sound asleep. With fear and trembling and a case of cottonmouth, I kneeled down beside my bed. I tried to control my breathing while my heart pounded. I mustered up more and more courage and whispered, "Lord, I come before your throne humbly yet boldly. I am not sure what the true answer is, but I know how I feel, Father God...Lord, I want to know if I am wrong for being gay? Is this who you made me in light of your vision, Lord?" I paused, took a deep breath, and felt a great weight lifted from my entire being. I continued, "Lord, I ask these things in your most precious and holy name. In Jesus name, I pray. Thank God. Amen."

I continued kneeling for a few minutes expecting an answer any minute. My thoughts went back to what Pastor Joyner touched on earlier. His words echoed in my head as I arose to lie down to sleep. To my surprise, the floor beneath my bed didn't open up revealing a place of fire and brimstone Christian folk say is for people like me. I had the most peaceful week I can remember. I had my answer because something changed in my being. I felt secure in the person I was becoming. I started writing and keeping a journal of my thoughts and poetry. Since I still felt like the only gay guy in school, it was nothing for me to dwell in solitude. Even though I still worried about someone discovering "my secret," I admitted to myself that I was no longer different. I was simply gay. This person was no longer someone living inside of himself. He had a presence, he had a face, he was made in His image, and his name was Jason...

Just as I was becoming comfortable with myself, my biggest fear was realized. "My secret" was discovered and uncovered when my mom found the journal I'd been keeping. I laugh about it now as an adult, but it wasn't so funny back then. I still wonder what went through her head as she read some of the pages. Hell, how much of it did she read? My journal was filled with my inner most thoughts and fantasies of my first kiss with a guy, my erotic desires of the things I would do to him sexually if I had a chance; I wrote about kats I had crushes on, but before all of that, I am certain her first shocking moment was when she read the first page embossed with the bold proclamation, "I'm Gay! There I said it."

My world changed after my secret was exposed. Suddenly, instinctively, I knew I had to fend for myself. I didn't want my parents holding anything over my head because of how they felt about homosexuality. I had to map out my own plan, which wasn't hard due to my independent nature. I love my parents unconditionally, but this was an area where unconditional love on their part would not manifest itself. My dad didn't really have much to say once my mom revealed the discovery she had made in my room on my bed. My daddy always had something to say, whether it was a joke or something profound. I looked up to my dad and admired many of the sacrifices he made for the family. He always expressed himself verbally, physically, and humbly. However, he couldn't find the words to say what and how he truly felt the day he found out his son was gay.

My dad was the all American highly decorated soldier- a "man's man," the epitome of a strong black man. How could his seed produce someone deemed "soft," "a punk," "weak," – "less than a man?" I assumed this is what he thought. Perhaps he felt that this was punishment from God for some wrong turns he may have made in life. God telling him, "Now deal with that..."

I decided to join the Navy after graduation. It wasn't the path my dad wanted me to take, but he knew this was a choice about which I was adamant. My parents drove me to the recruiter station in Ramstein, Germany. We talked the whole way and enjoyed a really nice lunch. They watched me finalize paper work and the official swearing-in. I was excited. I wasn't scared at all. There were kats crying and junk, but I had this smile on my face. I felt a new level of independence, more so than I ever felt before. For the first time in a long while, I knew things were going to be all right. I knew that I was making the right decision for me. As a man, I think my dad knew how I was feeling. We shared a laugh and a father/son embrace when they dropped me off at the hotel after we left the recruiting station. When I turned towards my mom she smiled and instructed me to "Be careful." It was one of the most memorable times for me because she told me she loved me. My mother could be a bit detached emotionally, and at times, it is hard to decipher what she is thinking or how she feels about a given situation. One emotion that she exudes quite well and without question is that of anger when she dislikes or is upset about something, but that day at that moment her feelings were crystal clear. She doesn't say it often, so when she does, it's always refreshing and reassuring at the same time. I guess she didn't totally hate me. When we hugged, it felt like she didn't want to let me go. In that moment, I wished I could take back one thing - the day she discovered I was gay! I didn't want her to find out the way she did; the coming out story I had imaged was completely different! It was bittersweet when the three of us parted ways. I later found out from my dad that she cried in the car on the way back home. I wish I could have seen that. I have never seen that woman cry.

Maybe that's from whom I get my stoic and hardcore nature. "Tough love" was her motto. And I would learn the hard way that love was indeed tough...

The next day my recruiter woke me up with a call and met me outside the hotel room. He treated me to breakfast, gave me my first set of orders, and my airline tickets back to the U.S. He dropped me off at the airport, and I was on my way to my new life. I continued to reflect on the past year and imagined all the possibilities ahead of me. I was so anxious that I couldn't sleep on my long flight back. When I did finally doze off, I dreamt of the previous Christmas I had with my family. I went all out that year, working hard and spending every dime I had on the gifts I got my parents and sister. I wanted to let them know how much I loved and appreciated them. In my mind, it felt like it would be my last holiday with them, so I wanted to make sure I brought a little something special to the season, so they'd remember me, knowing that things hadn't changed all that much; I was still their son, their brother...although I was gay. I wished they could walk a mile in my shoes to know what I went through and why I had to distance myself thousands of miles away from them in order to find me...

Meet and Greet

Boot camp was a trip! There were a lot of yelling and mind games, which didn't intimidate or frighten me. My biggest fear during those nine weeks? – Getting a hard on in the shower from looking at all those phyne-ass kats, but to my surprise, at the end of the day, sex was the last thing on my mind. However, I did have fantasies in my sleep or during the day, but with all the running around, training exercises, and studying naval knowledge and history, I only wanted to get clean and get as much sleep as possible. I always looked forward to the training coming to a close for the day. After boot camp, I was off to Dental Technician school in Wichita Falls, Texas, and then to Camp Pendleton, California, for Field Medical Service School to learn how to treat patients, provide first aid, and perform triage operations in a combat zone. Six months later, I was given orders to Okinawa, Japan. So once again, I was back overseas feeling like the odd man out, really wanting to be stateside; I had already spent four years overseas in Europe with my folks.

My time in Japan was like high school all over again – hiding who I was, making up excuses as to why I wasn't trying to holler at the girls who showed interest in me, and putting up a façade in the locker room when it came time to discuss the male conquest of "the chicken head." I was like, "Lord, why can't I just be normal, so that I can at least enjoy hanging out with my straight colleagues." I thought, I should just come out and be done with it, but I didn't want to give up like that, so I did my time and actually started to enjoy my tour in Japan. I would hang out with my shipmates from time to time if I wasn't in a college class. I tried to blend in as much as possible to survive. In addition to my job, which I loved, I got to work alongside the Marines. The year I spent there was both challenging and rewarding; however, I built a great camaraderie with the unit and learned that in life you have to play the game. Sometimes you just have to fake it to make it...

My next set of orders took me to Camp Lejeune, North Carolina, just outside the boring and lifeless town of Jacksonville. Ironically, it was in this lifeless town that I began to find my life. Even though there was little to do in the surrounding area, I was grateful to be stateside again, and excited too, for it was time to play *hard!* After about a month of being stuck on the base and bumming rides, I bought a car. I saved up quite a bit of change during my stay in Japan. I love sports cars, and I found a really good deal on one of my dream cars at a tent sale. It was an immaculate red Nissan 300ZX. It had tan leather and every option imaginable. Best of all, it was a stick. I had one of my supervisors show me the ropes of a manual transmission. As any service member on any military installation will tell you, having a reliable car means freedom. With my own ride, I sought to meet some like-minded individuals - namely some cool gay guys with whom I could hit the streets. As luck would have it, I met my first set of gay friends at a small get together my co-worker Leyah was throwing.

When Leyah and I met, we hit it off, especially when we discovered we were both originally from the Midwest. She was from East St. Louis, and I represent Detroit. Leyah was light skinned with a thick head of naturally sandy brown hair. I thought she was pretty. She was somewhat of a ghetto girl, but she was a lot of fun to be around and very precocious in her demeanor. Leyah had developed a little crush on me initially, and I reluctantly had to let the cat out of the bag. One night after a movie, I guess she decided I wasn't moving fast enough for her taste, and she took it upon herself to back me into a corner and kiss me. I wasn't expecting it, and it freaked me out. I was under the impression that we had a mutual understanding that we were two friends going to the movies. Now that she knows I like men, she always asks, "When you gon' let me convert you?" I thought telling her I was gay was going to be the deal breaker, but that only fueled her fire, especially when I told her I had never been with a female. Rekindling a relationship with one of her old boyfriends kept me off hook. Seeing her interact with him made me want to get a boyfriend of my own. Nevertheless, Leyah and I became great friends, and the invitation to her small get together could not have come at a better time. It had been a hellacious week at work. Our clinic had undergone a major command inspection where everything from staff, clinical functions, knowledge, and our facility was put under the microscope, to determine just how well we were delivering quality healthcare. It was time to blow off some steam and relax....

I didn't know what to expect about going to Leyah's gathering. She always kept me on my toes. In my head, I was thinking, "Is this broad going to have a candlelight dinner waiting for me? Is she planning to get me drunk and try to convert me? I laughed as I played the scenario out in my mind. It tripped me out that she was trying to turn me from being gay in her own right, yet was so gay friendly. When she told me the story of her upbringing, it all made sense. Her aunt who raised her was a lesbian. She took custody of her as a minor after her mother passed away while giving birth to her baby brother. She said there was always a card party at her aunt's on the weekends, and she would always have her gay friends over. Leyah became very comfortable with them, so much so that she became a magnet for gay men and lesbians. Her first sexual encounter was with her aunt's girlfriend's 16-year-old son, who was questioning his sexuality. He wanted to "test the waters" by being with a girl. The two of them went all the way, and she claims that it was so good, his confusion turned to a desire for females. Her crazy butt told me that her pussy could do the same for me. I was like, "Girl, I'm not questioning nor am I confused."

I made my way down her block and parked in the driveway. There were other cars parked in front of her house, so my suspicions perhaps were wrong. As I made my way to the door, I could hear laugher and music playing. I knocked loudly so that I would be heard. A few moments later, Leyah appeared.

"Williams, what's up, Boy?" Leyah asked.

"Nothing, Girl, what's up?" I replied.

"Come on in, Pookie," she said. She gave me a tight embrace making sure I could feel the softness of her breasts. I shook my head as she let me into her home. She had a smile from ear to ear on her face. "You're lucky my man is in town."

"Oh really?" I laughed nervously. I wasn't the least bit surprised at her blatant flirting.

She grabbed my hand and yelled out, "Craig, turn that shit up nigga! Oooh, that's my shit!" The track, "Oochie Wally," bumped louder in the background. She started popping her booty to the bass line. I laughed as she led me inside.

"You want something to drink, eat, smoke? Cigarettes that is," she laughed. I just looked at her and smiled.

"I'm cool for now. I'll get something later. What have you had to drink?"

"Just a lil' bit of Rum and Coke. You don't drink, do you?"

"I haven't really ventured down that road since Okinawa. It's a long story," I said. She let my hand go as we came upon two fellas sitting on the couch.

"These are Craig's homies. That's Jamal and that's

13

Kenny." I did a little head nod, and we continued. "It's still early, so not er'ybody I told to come is here yet. My friends I was telling you about the other day are coming, so don't be trying to dip out all early and shit."

I laughed and sat down on the loveseat. Leyah walked back towards the kitchen and came back with a bottle of Sprite for me. This tall attractive brown skinned dude followed in behind her. He walked up to me and gave me the standard "brotha man" handshake. His hand seemed to swallow mine as he firmly gripped it making his presence known.

"I'm Craig, bruh. What's up?"

"What's going on man?" I smiled thinking to myself, *DAMN! You are too phyne to be straight.* The picture Leyah showed me of him didn't capture the extent of his good looks.

"You got it, dawg." He turned towards Leyah and scooped her up in his arms. "I'm 'bout to head out baby? Yo' ass better behave," he said tapping her forehead with his index finger.

"Boy, you crazy. Bye, boo," she cooed. She stood on the tips of her toes and kissed his sexy full lips. He let her go and proceeded to walk out of the living room. "You need anything else, Jason?" she asked turning her attention to me.

"No, I'm good for now," I said as the two guys got up and headed out of the living room.

"Kayla, ya'll cool?" Leyah yelled. She grabbed the remote control and turned the music down.

"We cool!" this beautiful dark skinned girl said walking from the back of Leyah's crib. She wore this short flirty white tennis skirt with a green wife beater cut asymmetrically across the mid-section. Her hair was long, falling down past her shoulders, framing her face and accenting her lovely cat gray eyes. She extended her hand with sexy feminine grace and told me her name was Kayla. This short haired female who was dressed in baggy jeans, a throwback jersey, and Timbs followed behind her and sat on the couch. Kayla sat in her lap, and said, "Baby, this is Jason. Jason, this is my baby Jade."

"What's going on, dawg?" Jade replied in a voice deeper than mine.

"Nothing much, nice to meet ya'll," I replied observing Jade's haircut. Not only was her voice deeper than mine, but her fade looked better than mine as well. I made a mental note to ask her about her barber. She had a feminine face but could definitely pass for a dude at quick glance. I'm sure this was part of her sex appeal with the ladies.

"How long you been out here?" Jade asked.

"A couple of months," I replied.

"You a Marine?" Kayla asked.

"No, I'm in the Navy. I'm a Dental Tech."

"Oh, so you a Devil Doc? That's cool. How you like that?" Jade asked. (Devil Doc is a term that Marines use for anyone working in the Medical field. Marines affectionately called one another Devil Dog).

15

"I like it so far. Nothing to complain about yet."
"Right, right," Jade said.

"You two are Marines?" I asked.

"Oh hell naw! Jade is the soldier. I am too cute to camp in somebody's forest. Ah ah! I'm one of the managers at the Sprint Store on Western, so if you need a hook up come holler at'cha girl," Kayla replied in a cute southern accent. I smiled laughing at her countryness.

"So, where they got you stationed?" Jade asked.

"New River," I replied only to have everyone's attention grabbed by a loud,

"Heeeeyyy BITCH! The girls are here honey!" This feminine yet masculine sounding voice screeched from outside the front door.

I sipped my Sprite and turned around and saw Leyah letting in three guys. The one who yelled was tall, dark skinned, well-manicured, but not someone I could see myself dating. He wore a red wave cap that was so tight his eyes looked chinky. He was draped in a red Nautica t- shirt with the word Nautica encrusted in rhinestones, a pair of semi baggy jeans with fringes cut into the bottom of the legs, and a pair of tan Durango boots. This was Lyzell. He seemed very confident and very out and outgoing to say the least based on his grand entrance. A second guy, who was attractive, dark skinned, my height, followed behind him. He had a beautiful smile, and wore a Nautica jean jacket with the collar flipped up. He also wore a wife beater, jeans, and

16

Timbs and his name was Shawn. Before I even knew his name, I could tell Shawn and I would be in each other's life for a long while; I just had that feeling. His demeanor and personality were very magnetic. The next guy was a bit taller than me, wore a green polo shirt, and fitted cap and jeans, with Timbs. He was light skinned with light brown eyes and curly hair. I thought he was a cute dude initially. His name was Michael – a southern boy from Atlanta, Georgia, who appeared to be free spirited with mad sex appeal. Finally, there was Preston, a hip and very fashion forward, good looking brown skinned brotha. He was wearing a tapered cranberry button down shirt, with the sleeves neatly rolled up and a neckerchief in the breast pocket. He sported a fedora and fitted leather pants with matching boots. He was short in stature standing about 5'4." Preston was cute as a button and very much a southern gentlemen hailing from New Bern, North Carolina.

"What's the tea, bitch?" Leyah asked Lyzell as she laughed and hugged him. Shawn, Preston, and Michael hugged her and said hello as well.

"Ya'll come on and let's get crunk! I got some wings, liquor, and all that in the kitchen, so whatever is in there, have at it!"

"Girl, you ain't got to tell me twice," Lyzell said as he turned towards Shawn with this mean look on his face and proclaimed. "We bought some Smirnoff Ice. I gave this late girl some coins earlier to get some ALCOHOL BITCH, and this ho' buys Smirnoff Ice. Late and tired queen honey... LATENESS!"

"Oh girl, Miss Smirnoff gets me right where I need to be, honey. Don't do it girl! You might want to keep it cute and get into it. I can't do all those extras you other kids do. Chile, ya'll cuts up, honey," Shawn exclaimed!

"Chile cheese, honey. Take this late mess in the kitchen, girl. Let me see what Miss Leyah burned up tonight honey. You know she still learning how to cook, girl."

"Lyzell, not tonight!" Leyah laughed. "Jason, come here. These are the guys I was telling you about." I got up from my seat. "This is big mouth Lyzell. This is Michael, ol' cute self. This is my short little pookie bear Preston. And that was Shawn who went in the kitchen. Shawn, come meet my boy Jason I was telling ya'll about." I was slightly startled and developed a sudden case of nervousness when Leyah called my name. I walked over feeling my heart rate increase. All I could think about was not tripping and embarrassing myself.

"Hey!" Lyzell, Preston, and Michael said. In nervous laughter, I said hello and shook their hands. Shawn came out of the kitchen with a plate of wings and spaghetti and shook my hand.

"What's up?" Shawn said.

"Nothing man," I replied taking a gulp of my soda. "Oh, Miss Leyah made Spaghetti!" Lyzell pointed out.

"So you learned how to boil water, bitch? Jason, be careful with this ho's cooking; she likes to cook pots and carrying on for dinner." Shawn, Leyah, and I laughed.

"Shut your ass up! I forgot the pot was on the stove. See, what had happened was, I was trying to boil some noodles, and went to answer the phone and..."

Lyzell looked at me and interjected. "So we cackling on the phone, exchanging tea and carrying on, and next thing you know I hear, 'BEEP BEEP BEEP BEEEP!' Chile, her smoke detector is blaring, you hear me? And this ho calls out to JESUS! So I assume at this point she's running to the kitchen. She then tells me that the pot is melting and on fire, chile!!!!!! She's all hysterical. The noodles are on fire! I'll call you back! She done boiled all the water out the pot. Chile, that was a kee kee to me! I cackled something un-godly!" he said as we joined him in laughter.

"Leyah, you didn't smell smoke?" I asked, taking a sip of my Sprite.

"No, but I can cook got-dammit! Stop telling folks my business, boy!" Leyah said as she hit Lyzell in the chest. I smiled and tried to contain my nervousness. I was trying to figure out how to act.

"She had a cold, chile, so she says she couldn't smell the smoke. Fish honey! They are a Kee KEEE!" Lyzell screeched. "Chile, let me go see what miracle she done performed in this kitchen. Get me a few fierce wings honey, fill this belly! The girls are hungry! Michael, you want a cocktail girl?" Lyzell asked walking into the kitchen. I stood there wondering what he meant by the term kee kee. I wanted to ask, but my brain was screaming: DON'T SAY ANYTHING STUPID!

"Of course! I didn't drive, so make me something strong!"

"Lyzell, bring me one too!" yelled Shawn.

"A Smirnoff, bitch!" Lyzell yelled back.

"No, bitch, a cocktail!"

"I heard you ho, A Smirnoff!"

"A COCKTAIL, WHORE!"

"Okay lateness! Smirnoff it is!"

"That bitch tries it every chance she gets!" Shawn laughed, looking over at me.

"What happened?" Lyzell asked. "Nothing, girl!"

"Oh you would want to keep it cute, honey," Lyzell stated as he walked out handing Shawn a bottle of Smirnoff Ice, "cause you know I reads the late girls for blood, honey. This was a waste of my good hard earned coins." Lyzell then notices the androgynous Jade. "Hey Jade, girl, I mean boy, man!" Preston Chuckled to himself as he made his way further into the living room.

"What's up, dawg?"

"Chile, if you were a real boy, I might let you play in this pussy for a while, honey!"

"I'm straight, dawg," Jade said waving her hand in the air and smiling in a nonchalant manner seemingly ignoring Lyzell's comment.

"Are you? Kayla got her a man, bitch. I ain't mad honey," Lyzell said as he turned to walk back into the kitchen.

"Miss Kayla and Jade, how are ya'll? This ho' is beat

to meet Jesus, ain't she? Look at this girl work that skirt," Preston stated complimenting Kayla's clothes as he went over to hug her. "Very well done."

"Thank you. Preston, I like them pants," Kayla said. "The Gap, girl! Michael let me use his discount. I'm trying out something different," he said.

"You still work there, Mikey?"

"Yes, ma'am! They workin' me to death to be a part timer, do you hear me? I just put on third too, so the hospital decided to give me the A.L.P.O. spot in sick-call girl."

"A.L.P.O.? What's that?" Kayla asked.

"Assistant Leading Petty Officer –like an assistant manager in the civilian sector."

"Oh, so you the head bitch in charge?"

"Yes, ma'am. I might let the Gap go. I ain't decided yet. That mall discount is TOO nice."

Michael then turned his attention to me. "So Jason, how you like the great town of Jacksonville? Where they got you?" I took a deep breath cleared my throat and proceeded to answer his question. I was less nervous now that I was sitting down.

"It's boring so far, but it looks like you all make it work. I'm out at New River," I said noticing that all eyes were on me. I nervously took a drink forcing a smile.

"Oh that's cute, I like that base. You at the clinic or with the Air wing?"

"I'm at the clinic with Leyah," I said. As I studied his face, I noticed a scar half an inch in length above his left

21

eye. It added to his mystique and made me wonder about him.

"Oh yeah, you're a Dental Tech - not a Corpsman. I work at the hospital. I couldn't deal with that drive every morning. What's it like, twenty minutes?"
"Yeah almost...It's not too bad," I said.

"Oh, so you wouldn't be able to hang out with us for lunch, huh?" Shawn asked.

"No, I guess not, man," I said looking in his general direction. I was starting to loosen up a bit at that point, but I was still nervous mind you because I was now the focus of attention.

"So anyway, girls, ya'll not gon' be ready!" Lyzell screamed as he came out of the kitchen with a huge plate of food in one hand and two cocktails in the other. He handed one of the drinks to Michael, gave Preston the bottled water he held under his arm, and prepared to change the subject in his favor.

"Ready for what, chile?" Kayla asked.

"When I bust through in Miss Pathfinder, honey! Serving trade girl!"

"Trade Lyzell?" Shawn said as we all laughed. Lyzell rolled his eyes. I laughed knowing that there was no way in hell Lyzell would ever be able to be mistaken for the hyper masculine gay man trading sexual favors for money or gifts, but yet does not identify himself as being gay. Lyzell!?! Trade?!?! Please!!!!!!!

"Anyway, since the girls are making Sergeant coins now, I can cut up. The girls don' moved out the barracks, so now I'ma get Miss Mazda bashed and come back with a fierce new Pathfinder, honey."

"Ya'll Virginia kids know ya'll some stunt queens," Michael said, shaking his head and waving a finger in the air.

"Oh. Miss Michael, don't do it! Because you crafty ATL girls pull stunts without fail. Refresh my memory. How did you get those pants for Miss Girl over there, honey?" he said pointing at Preston.

"He paid for these, ho' - not to mention I get a mall discount, so don't come for me. Stuntin' is thievery bitch!!!" Michael hissed!

"Two-fifty for a pair of leather pants? Didn't the tag say a hundred seventy-five, girl?" Lyzell quipped as he and Shawn laughed and slapped each other high five. Preston shook his head and joined in on the laughter.

"That's a fierce discount, girl," Preston squealed. I chuckled to myself thinking why the hell they kept calling each other girl. That's not cool.

"You just make sure your airbag deploy, bitch! How about that!" Michael commented sharply. Everyone in the room broke out in laughter. I was taken aback by his comment, but realized it was all in playful love.

"AH LORD! Yes, make sure your airbag deploys! Chile, kee kee," Shawn said in between laughs.

"You tried it, Mike! You know I'm coming through there tomorrow. Be at the register, bitch!"

"You know I got my friends!" Michael said as he and Lyzell slapped each other high five. "Bitch, you tried it coming for Atlanta like that."

"Oh, girl, then don't give Virginia too much!" Shawn said.

"That's my sista, with her cheap leather. No, I'm serious bitch, two dollars and fifty cents? Girl, you showed up and showed out!" he said looking at Preston.

"KEE KEE!" Shawn piped in. After listening to these guys for a time, I finally figured out what a "kee-kee" was— something funny or ridiculous.

"Lyzell, you really gon' crash your car?" Leyah asked seemingly trying to figure out how he was going to do that. I was curious to know myself.

"I'm not, bitch. This trade piece is gon' do it for me. I let him play in this pussy a few times honey, and he works at this garage back home. He said he could get some of his boys to do it for me." I sat in amazement at Lyzell's colorful and animated banter. Now he was referring to his male parts as female parts. Note to self: You will not be doing that Jason. Ever in life! I let out a slight chuckle.

"Chile, that's a lot. Ya'll know this ho is serious, right?" Shawn questioned panning the room and pointing at us all.

"Oh yes, ma'am Pam. I'm serious girl. Speaking of having, let me use your 'puter girl." He got up from his seat and sashayed over to the computer desk. "I gotta chat this date, honey. See what the tea is, girl!" He muttered under his breath. He then turned in Leyah's direction and blurted out, "You paid AOL this month, girl?"

"Yeah, just turn the monitor on and SHET EP! Trying to be funny," Leyah said, rolling her eyes and then taking a sip of her cocktail.

"Can you see that big queen in a SUV?" Shawn whispered to me. We both laughed. I thought to myself, well he is tall, maybe he needs the room. What is the big deal, oblivious to the underlying read in Shawn's comment.

"You got a man, Jason?" Lyzell said. He looked over at me and gave me a beauty pageant wave and a smile perhaps hinting that he was available.

"Nope, I'm single," I proclaimed. Suddenly I panicked, hoping he wasn't coming on to me. Should I have said yes, I thought?

"I'ma find me and you a date or two or three," he smiled slyly and spun around to face the monitor. The long do-rag he was wearing flipped around like a girl's ponytail. He grabbed the tail end and started twirling it around his finger.

"Alright," I said laughing. I looked at him wondering if I should tell him what I was attracted too.

"Eh heh. What are you a pocketbook or a wallet, honey?" he asked me as he continued logging onto the website.

"What?" I asked in a puzzled tone, unclear of what he meant.

"Are you a pitcher or a catcher? Boy or a girl, honey. Top or bottom?" He asked in several different ways to make sure that I understood after swinging around in the chair to face me. He smiled and batted his eyes. Everyone in the room either laughed or shook their heads at Lyzell. When I opened my mouth to speak, everyone was looking in my general direction.

"Oh, I'm a...,"

"LYZELL! Shawn interjected, grabbing my leg and quickly shushing me. He looked at Lyzell as if to say you've taken this far enough. "Jason, you do not have to answer that. Chile, you are a kee-kee!" Shawn said, laughing. Lyzell just laughed as he logged onto CollegeClub.com.

These guys seemed like a lot of fun. I shared some laughs and survived my first adventure of gay world. The conversations were so colorful, and I slowly learned the lingo. They were using all kinds of code words. Some I had seen in E. Lynn Harris and James Earl Hardy novels. I wanted to hang out with them, but I was like, "Oh my God, are they this flamboyant in public?" I guess I would have to test the waters with caution. I mean I was in the military, and we were in this small town. Plus, I wasn't sure how "gay" I was. Is there a limit? I was trippin' because I couldn't believe Shawn and especially Lyzell were both Marines. With all the "honeys," "chiles," and "girls" being spoken, I wondered how they spoke and acted in the workplace. I knew I wasn't going to be *that* gay, but they were in the Marines. The first thought that comes to mind is a tough bad boy who's a trained killer for the country. I guess *we* are everywhere. Later I found out they both had admin jobs. Go figure. It seemed if anything I could count on them for a good laugh and a fashion tip or two from Preston.

Before everyone parted ways that night, I exchanged numbers with Michael, Lyzell, Preston, and Shawn. Shawn invited me to hang out with them the next day. I agreed to meet them around one in the afternoon. As I drove home, I chuckled to myself thinking about the night's events. It was quite a sight listening to them talk and interact. At times, it was like watching a comedy special on cable – a gay version of *Def Comedy Jam*. I got to my barracks room a little around 1:30 in the morning. My roommate was sound asleep. I quietly undressed, brushed my teeth, and slipped into bed. I couldn't wait to see what the next day would bring.

Karaoke in the Car

I woke up to the sound of my phone ringing. I rubbed my eyes and grabbed it off of my nightstand to see who it was. I looked at the caller I.D. It read Shawn. My first thought was, "Who the hell is Shawn?" Then memories from last night hit me. I almost forgot that I had given him my number. I quickly flipped opened the phone and uttered a hello.

"Hey, Jason, this is Shawn. How you doing?" I rubbed my eye and repositioned the phone.

"I'm good, man, what's going on?" I asked yawning

"Nothing, I didn't wake you, did I?" He chuckled. I could hear water running in the background.

"Oh, man, naw, it's cool," I lied sort of wishing I was still sleep. "I need to get up." I looked at the clock. It was 12:17. I looked over across the room and saw that my roommate was gone. His bunk was neatly made. I quickly got up and drew the shade open to let some light into the room.

"Okay, cool. You up?" Shawn laughed, trying to feel out my situation.

"Yeah," I yawned.

"Did you still want to hang out today? Me and Lyzell were gonna go to the mall and probably get something to eat," he said fishing for confirmation.

"Yeah, I still want to go. Of course, I need to shower and stuff," I said giving my underarm a sniff. I yawned and stretched my legs.

"Okay! I do too. I can come get you, and you can ride with me to Lyzell's. Where are your barracks?"

"I'm across from the Field House - in the Dental Barracks, right across from our headquarters building. Like, if you go around the circle, I'm in those barracks on the right side coming out of the circle," I said gesturing the explanation to myself.

"Oh, you're not far from me. I can look out the window and see your barracks. That's right across the street. I'm in H&S barracks."

"Oh okay cool, I know where you are. Well, I'm in room 114 over here. I said walking over to look out of the window.

"Alright, so it's like 12:20ish now so I will see you in about... um...an hour? Is that cool?"

"Yeah, that'll work."

"Okay see you in a few."

"Okay, bye."

"Bye."

I ran to the bathroom to relieve myself, washed my hands, and scrambled to my wall locker to pick out some clothes. I then set the iron and ironing board up. I turned on the stereo and popped in Tamia's new CD. I selected Track number 3, and hummed along to the chorus of, "I Can't Go for That." I ironed my clothes and sort of wondered how I should dress. I was more or less thinking how Shawn and them would be dressed. I was a simple dude. A nice pair of stylish jeans, a tee shirt, and a fresh pair of sneaks was my thing. I walked over to the door and opened it. It was a breezy day, so I made a mental note to bring a jacket. The sun was out and leaves were blowing through the parking lot. I closed the door and continued getting ready. Around 1:50, my phone rang.

"Hey, what's up Shawn?" I smiled.

"I'm pulling up in the parking lot now. What room is it again?"

"One-fourteen. I'm walking outside now." I looked to my left and saw a red car easing through the parking lot. I assumed it was him, so I made my exit through the door and waved.

"Okay. Oh, I see you," he said. We hung up. I turned to lock my door, and walked up to his car and got in. I was pretty cool; no nervous tension reared its ugly head just yet. I think I was more comfortable with Shawn than the other guys. He had a calm spirit about him this afternoon.

"What's up?" He asked.

"Nothing, man, what's going on?" I grabbed the seatbelt and wrapped it across my torso. I relaxed in the seat and let out a long breath.

"Nothing much. We gotta go get Lyzell. I'm hungry though. I take it you didn't eat yet either?" he said glancing over in my direction. He turned the radio volume down a few pegs.

"Naw, I had just woke up when you called," I said. I looked over at him and stated, "I was just listening to this CD," pointing at the radio.

"Okay! She did that. I like that song "Love Me in a Special Way," that's my song," he said as he moved his head to the beat of the song playing.

"I like that one too, and that one she got with Missy," I said smiling and tapping my fingers on my leg.

"Yeah, that one is cute too."

"So, how long are you stationed out here?" he asked.

"I'm here for two years. What about you?" I asked looking out of the window at some Marines in PT shorts running.

"I'll be here for four. I've done two and a half years already," he said nodding his head. He glanced over at me and then behind me so that he could switch lanes.

"You like it?" I asked, wondering what motivated him to join the toughest of all military branches.

"Umm, it has its moments. I don't plan on making this a career. Lyzell and me joined together. We're best friends from back home. I did a year of college and found out I wasn't really ready to go to school." He paused and looked over at me shaking his head. "And that chile convinced me to join with him. We were joking around one day, and we ended up challenging one another to see who would actually sign up to be a Marine. And oddly enough, here we are." He laughed and took one hand off of the steering wheel before continuing. "We always have to outdo one another. See who'll outdo who!"

32

"That's a trip. So ya'll were a part of the buddy system?" I asked, wondering if they were in the same unit in boot camp.

"Yeah, what about you?" he asked, coming to a stop at the red light. An elderly couple on bikes rode past across the intersection. My eyes followed them as they made it safely to the other side.

"I joined the Navy because I felt I was going to waste my dad's money and flunk out of college. I wanted to do something on my own," I said gleaming with self-sufficient pride.

"Oh wow, not flunk out," he chuckled.

"Yeah, I didn't feel like I was ready for that among other things, plus the whole gay thing," I said without saying too much while having a brief flashback of the day I was outed.

"I get it. I did a year of college before I joined though. I wasn't ready, so I understand where you're coming from," Shawn said. "So, how you like the Navy?"

"It's cool so far. I don't know about Jacksonville though," I smiled allowing my facial expression to place emphasis on the words.

"Okay!" He let out a loud giggle. "We usually go home on the weekend, but I didn't feel like driving, and that chile had duty Friday. So here we are in Latesonville!" he said shaking his head.

"Ya'll from Virginia, right?" I asked, trying to recall if that's where he told me he was from or not.

"Yup, Chesapeake, Virginia...born and raised. It's

like about four hours from here," he said glancing over his shoulder to switch lanes.

"Cool," I said reading the marquee of one of the furniture shops monthly specials as we passed by.

"Where you from?" he asked changing the track on the CD.

"Originally Detroit, Michigan - the Motor City baby," I said in a you'd-better-recognize tone.

"Oh cool. I've never been up there," he said taking a pause and letting out a, hmmm. "You should come home with us one weekend. We probably gon' go again next weekend." He paused again, before continuing. "Um...yeah, that's a payday weekend, so yeah. You want to go? You twenty-one?" Shawn asked.

"Yeah, that would be cool," I said with excitement, "but, I don't turn twenty-one until January," I continued, wondering if I'd be able to get into the clubs at twenty?

"Okay. I turned twenty-one this past August," he said grinning proudly as if he were letting me know he was a man now.

"Cool, happy belated," I said.

"Thanks," he replied. "I think you can get in the club. They just give you a wristband. We used to use fake ID's for the longest."

"So what do ya'll do around here?" I said after a quick laugh. I wondered was going to the mall as good as it got in this town. I was already burnt out with that, but it would be great to have somebody to shop with, It

34

would also be a welcomed change in regard to being myself without the facade.

"Well, we just make up stuff to do, really. If we're not home, then we are hanging out at Lyzell's, Preston, or Leyah's place," Shawn explained. "Leyah is a kee kee," he smiled and looked over at me. "Sometimes we go to this club called Spectrum. I think we can get you into Spectrum too come to think of it. They barely check I.D's. Just show 'em your military I.D. and you will definitely get in. It's in Fayetteville, which is like two hours away. I don't know," he said shrugging his shoulders and taking a moment to swallow. "We just come up with stuff. You'll have fun hanging with us though. Oh, and later on we were gonna go to Lyzell's house to watch that new show, Queer as Folk. You heard of it?"

"I think I heard something about it," I said trying to recall. "I've been out of the states and stuff, so I'm still playing catch up on a lot of things."

"Oh, you were overseas?" he asked looking at me with curiosity.

"Yeah, Okinawa before I came here, and my dad is in the Army," I proudly stated. "I went to high school in Germany."

"Oh that's cool! Did you like it?"

"Yeah, but I was ready to be back in the States." As much as I loved being overseas, I felt like I had missed the incontrovertible American teenaged experience.

"Okay! I couldn't imagine being that far from home.

This is really the furthest I've ever been away from home."

"It's not bad, man. If you ever get a chance to go to Europe, go. I'm telling you." I couldn't relate to being in the same city or town due to my experiences with moving to a new place every two or three years. To me, the adventure was exciting. It fascinated me when I met people who were just leaving the small towns they grew up in.

"I will keep that in mind. Visiting yeah, but living there, I don't know, but yeah, that's cool," he said appearing to play with the idea of living abroad. Queer as Folk is the first openly gay series on Showtime. Most of the cast is supposed to be gay in real life and the first show came on last Sunday. It was so good. I got life!" he said with resonating joy.

"What does that mean?" I asked. I became amused each time I heard one of them use that phrase.

"Oh that's like saying you really enjoyed something. You say, I got life! Or you can say I got my LIFE!" he said and let out a little laugh.

"Oh okay, I get it now. I got life!" I repeated. I let out a laugh as I mocked and imitated his voice the way he'd said it.

"Ooooh. We're gonna rub off on you. You ready?" he laughed.

"I don't know," I said laughing again. "You all are a trip to me. I don't know if I can hang, especially with Lyzell. He is over the top," I said shaking my head in amazement. I was still in awe of his actions and mannerisms. Images of him from the night before went through my head.

"That big ol' queen is harmless," Shawn chuckled. "Just let him have it a few times, and you two will be the best of friends," he said laughing.

"Do ya'll always call each other girl?" I asked laughing. Shawn thought for a second before answering.

"Yeah, I guess so. It's like a term of endearment." He thought for a second before continuing. "Shit, I don't even notice when I say it anymore."

"Oh okay, I don't know about all that," I said shaking my head no and smiling.

"You think we're too gay, huh?" he asked.

"I didn't say that. I am sure there are kats gayer than ya'll. It was just a trip to see ya'll interact last night. It was like I was watching something on T.V. I couldn't stop laughing at ya'll." I had countless laughs under my breath so as not to be rude.

"Yeah, that's just us joking around. You got to have fun with your friends or what's the point?" Shawn said laughing as we made a right turn into a residential area.

"Yeah, that's true, but ya'll seem cool. It's nice to have someone take me under their wing. I'm still new to this," I said with a shoulder shrug.

"Awwww, we got you," he said giving me thumbs up, "and Michael thought you were cute by the way. Don't tell him I told you that."

I laughed as we pulled up in front of Lyzell's townhouse. Shawn called Lyzell and told him we were outside. Lyzell emerged five minutes later and walked towards the car. I opened the passenger door and moved the seat forward to get in the back of the car. Lyzell got in the car and closed the door.

"Hey, Jason. What's going on cunt?" he said looking at me and then turning in Shawn's direction. "What's up?" I replied, again laughing at him under my breath. I could not wait to see how entertaining he'd be today.

"Hey, whore!" Shawn said in a high-pitched voice. I laughed at the two of them.

"Let's hit it girls!" Lyzell yelled. He reached over and buckled his seatbelt.

"Hit it!" Shawn hollered back chuckling as he put the car in reverse.

"Chile, I'm so tired of hearing, It's a stranger in my house, took a while to figure out..." Lyzell sang in an irritating voice. "Chile, put this in, girl." He grabbed his man bag and reached in to remove a CD case.

"Ah Lord! You don't like Tamia, chile," Shawn asked sounding disappointed. He ejected the disc and placed it in the CD holder over his visor.

"Chile, she carries me! You will wear a song out, honey!" Lyzell pointed at Shawn as he made his statement. He inserted a disc into the CD slot.

"You's a evil banshee whore! What is this, chile?" "The beats girl. I need to hear, 'The Ha,' so I can cut up bitch!" he said snapping his fingers and moving side-to-

38

side.

"You are a kee kee! That's that DJ Sedrik mix?" Shawn asked adjusting the volume.

"Uh huh! From a couple weeks ago. I stole it from Kyle. So what's up Jason, you ready to cut up with the girls?" Lyzell asked as he bounced to the house music.

"Yeah, ready to see what the day will bring!" I said. I was trying to figure out what the hell this music was playing. I was into all sorts of music, but this was definitely something new to me - True House music.

"YESSSS! Boy, don't waste my time! Just put your head between my THIGHS! Cuz I ain't got time for no GAMES! And if you AIN'T TYING TO EAT BOY DAT'S A SHAME! BA DA DA DA DA DA DA DA DA DA!"

Lyzell and Shawn sang in high pitch voices with the female singer and mocked the drumbeats. I sat back laughing. This was pure comedy to me! We made our way to the mall, and I was wondering how they were going to act. I was thinking please don't call attention to us by acting flamboyantly. I didn't know if I was that comfortable yet. I was still coming into my own. I decided not to trip, but rather go with the flow. Shawn parked, and we all got out.

"Remember your lines, girls," Lyzell whispered. "I don't want the kids to know my tea!" I chuckled to myself. Was he serious? The tea is they know your tea, I thought.

"Oh, chile, bye! You big late queen!" Shawn said bursting into laughter. He glanced over at me and observed me trying not to laugh. Lyzell just rolled his eyes and kept walking. As we entered the mall, I was again shocked at how small it was, but then I had to remember I was in a small town. We stopped into The Gap and met up with Michael who was folding jeans.

"Hey ya'll, what's up?" He greeted us once he saw us.

"Nothing much. Doing a little shopping," Lyzell said reaching over to hug him.

"Baby, they got me working like a slave up in here today. I should have left the party a little bit earlier last night," Michael said as he threw a pair of jeans over his left shoulder.

"You gon' be alright?" I asked feeling bad that he couldn't venture out with us.

"Yeah, I'll be fine," he said. "I complain about this every week. You'd think I'd act like it's my routine by now."

"You coming to the house tonight? We gon' get together and watch the Queers," Lyzell said.

"Yeah, I told Jesse. He wants to come, is that alright?" Michael asked awaiting approval.

"Of course! The more the merrier," Lyzell said. He snapped his fingers making a loud popping sound.

"Is he on the schedule today?" Shawn asked looking around the store.

"Yeah, he's in the back with some customers," he said turning his head towards the rear of the store. "Why did this white girl come in here looking a hot shitty mess. I haven't seen nobody in stretch pants with the lil' stirrups since grade school," he said in a hushed tone before we all laughed with him. "Tell me why they were dingy yellow, and she had on a yellow sweater that almost matched the pants, but not quite." He looked at me and continued. "Her belly was spilling out the side like an ice cream cone. And get this, she finished the look off with some green Keds. When I tell you I kee-kee'd." Michael smiled.

"I know you did," Shawn said laughing. They slapped each other high five.

"She looked like she was growing sunshine with her big ass," Michael added. We all burst into laughter again.

"Stop it," Lyzell said laughing. "Let me look around and see what I should purchase."

"We have some great sweaters on sale like the one I'm wearing." Michael said popping his collar. "Check those out. A blue one would look so good on you, Jason," Michael said as he turned toward me.

"Cool, I do need some sweaters," I said smiling and nodding my head.

"They're 30% off. So ya'll go look around. I need to re-do these mannequins. Let me know when ya'll ready, and I'll ring you guys up," he said as he returned to the part of the sales floor he was working.

Shawn and I walked around and both picked out a couple of sweaters. I was helping him pick out a pair of jeans when this tall dark skinned guy walked up to us and asked if we needed any assistance. Shawn turned and gave him a hug.

"What's going on, Jesse?" Shawn said smiling. He stepped back and leaned on the rack next to where we were standing.

"Nothing much, boy...just trying to get these people to spend their hard earned money. I noticed you and your friend here don't have enough merchandise hanging off of your arms, so I figured I should help you," Jesse said as he turned his head toward me flashing a bright smile.

I blushed. He was too cute. He had a clean-shaven face with dark chiseled features and a nice evenly toned build. He was about six feet tall, had dark brown almond shaped eyes, a low all even haircut, and a beautiful smile accented by a set of dimples. More importantly, he was masculine. I regained my composure as he extended his hand toward me and introduced himself.

"I'm Jesse. And you must be Jason?" he stated with obvious flirtation.

"Good guess," I said trying not to blush any more than I already had. I'm not sure if my attempt worked.

"Michael told me about you earlier today. I would have to agree with him," he said scanning my frame from head to toe.

"I'm sorry. Agree with what?" I asked puzzled.

"You are very attractive," he gushed.

"Thank you," I smiled blushing harder than ever,

showing my deep dimples (which was cool because I love showcasing them).

"No doubt, you're welcome," he said turning towards Shawn, who was smiling and shaking his head.

"So you coming over to Lyzell's tonight? We're going to watch Q.A.F.," Shawn asked shaking his head.

"Fo' show, we should be out of here before 7:00. I worked until close last night, so as soon as we close, I'm trying to run out of here, man." He looked over at me and smiled.

"Excuse me, sir, do you all have this in a small?" A woman asked interrupting.

"I'm sure we do. Let me check in the back. Do you mind waiting while I find out for you?" Jesse asked courteously.

"No, I don't mind," the woman replied.

"Okay guys, duty calls. I will get up with you guys later. Nice meeting you, Jason. Alright, Shawn," Jesse said as he walked to the storeroom.

"Oh my God!!! Shawn he is phyne as hell," I said finally unable to contain myself.

"Yeah, you have some dust bunnies on your tongue. It was hanging all out your mouth," he said laughing, tapping my chin.

"No, it wasn't," I laughed.

"That's cute though. I think he likes you. That's Michael's best friend."

"Who like who girl?" Lyzell piped in placing his arms around us.

"Jesse and Jason. Jesse was over here about to run game," Shawn stated.

"Well, you are the latest piece of ass in Jacksonville, girl." Lyzell said looking at me. "I hear he has a cock-a-saurus. You might get life! I'd chat him, but I love me some trade, honey," he said in a hushed tone. I just looked at him wondering what the hell he was talking about?

"Chile, you are a mess! Okay, I'm ready to go get something in this belly. Ya'll ain't hungry?" Shawn asked shifting the clothes in his arms.

"Yes!" Lyzell and I exclaimed. "Let's pay for this stuff and go to Golden Corral," Shawn suggested.

"Oh, I don't eat at buffets." I stated clearly shaking my head no.

"Oh, you one of them girls?" Lyzell stated.

"One of what girls?" I said now offended that he referred to me as a girl for the second time. I did not like that use of the word and eventually would have to let them know not to refer to me as girl.

"Bourgeois," he replied sucking his teeth.

"No, I just don't like buffets or cafeteria style food. It reminds me of the galley and stuff. All those people breathing and talking over everything, coughing, and touching the spoons. Then you don't know how long that food has been there being recycled. I would prefer not to eat at those types of restaurants," I said providing a sound explanation.

"Hmph! Well, say no more," Lyzell grunted. He

flared his nose up at me.

"Well, let's go to Applebee's, is that cool?" Shawn asked looking in my general direction.

"Yeah that's cool," I said nodding my head yes.

"Well, I did want a fierce yeast roll, but Miss Applebee's will be cute, honey. Chile!" Lyzell said waving a hand in the air.

"If it's that serious you guys can drop me off to my car, and I can go grab a bite someplace else. I mean I do have keys. And I can get up with ya'll later," I said, now irritated with Lyzell. I thought to myself, He and I had only known each other a day and we were already butting heads.

"Chile, don't mind me. Shawn girl she bites back, honey. That was cute for you," he said smiling at me. "You gets your tens across the board," Lyzell laughed and snapped his fingers. We proceeded to the checkout.

"Jason, don't worry about this big evil woman. We can go to Applebee's," Shawn stated trying to keep the peace going.

"This all ya'll are getting today?" Michael stated as he walked up to the register.

"Yeah, you got us girl?" Lyzell whispered.

"Um huh. What ya'll about to get into now?" Michael asked.

"About to go eat. I'm hungry."

"Chile you stay hungry," Michael said laughing.

"Hmph, I guess girl," Lyzell stated.

"So it's cool if I bring Jesse right? I know how you get about people in your house?" He paused for effect and then grabbed the scanner to ring up the items on the counter.

"Yeah, chile, just don't be vogueing and carrying on if my roommate come through the door. He went to see his family in South Carolina, but he should be back sometime tonight."

"Well, I don't plan on being over there late anyway. Tomorrow is a work day," Michael said.

"Okay! It is Monday tomorrow," Lyzell said.

Michael rang each of us up and gave us his discount. We walked out of the store, and Lyzell placed his arm over my shoulders and asked if I was mad at him. I shook my head no and turned to Shawn who was shaking his head.

"Good, since you're not mad and we're going to Applebee's, cocktails on me. You girls drink water with lemon, right?"

Shawn and I laughed as the three of us made our way out of the mall to the car. I had survived my first outing with the "girls." It wasn't as bad as I thought it would be. We proceeded to Applebee's and Shawn told me all about last week's episode of Queer as Folk, so that I wouldn't be totally lost when we watched the second episode. I was really looking forward to seeing what the show was about. I was also anticipating seeing Jesse again, but it wasn't Jesse who would soon capture my attention....

"Hello, how you doing, Ma?" I said answering my phone. I opened the car door to let some air inside before adjusting the phone.

"I'm okay. What are you doing?" she replied.

"I just got off work not too long ago. I'm sitting in the car about to go to the gym," I said leaning back in the seat. I placed the phone between my shoulder and ear and started rifling through my gym bag looking for my headphones.

"Oh yeah. Oh ya'll get off early on Friday?" she asked. It sounded as if she were washing dishes in the background.

"It depends on what's going on for the day. We do a half and half rotation, where half the staff is off for the day. The other half work but get a half a day or at least leave early depending on the work load." I located the headphones and placed them around my neck. I moved the bag over onto the passenger seat.

"Hmph. What else is going on? You been alright?"
"For the most part, I've been trying to adjust to this slow pace. It's like next to nothing to do out here," I said starring out of the window.

"Good, that means you can get your butt in school and utilize that time while you're out there. Have you enrolled or at least looked?" she said in a stern motherly tone.

"Kind of..." I said. I really didn't want to have this

conversation with her right now. Right now, my mind was focused on the weekend at hand.

"What does 'kind of' mean? No?" she said as I closed my eyes preparing myself for her to lecture. I was going to cut her off at the chase this time though.

"Naw, Ma," I laughed. "What I want to do is go to hygiene school. I have to put a package in for it though, but what I have to do first is take a microbiology and chemistry course. And then the command is sending me to an x-ray course for dental radiography. So I need to wait until that is over first, and then I can do my own thing."

"Well, don't wait forever," she warned.

"I won't, Ma... How is everybody?" I asked, thanking God for an opportunity to change the subject.

"They're alright. I'm going to kick your sisters behind though."

"Why? What happened?"

"She's sitting up here running behind this ugly lil' boy."

"She told me she was seeing some dude the last time I talked to her. She said he bought her a necklace or a ring or something. I forgot what she said. What's wrong with him?" I laughed. I looked at my fingernails and made a mental note to clip them later.

"He just stupid. He gon' come up to the house all late to pick the girl up for her little homecoming dance. He pulls up to the house and blew the damn horn. So you know your daddy went out there and made him come in the house. He all stuttering and lying about why he's late. Your daddy asked him if he was drunk." Mama started laughing. "He said, 'No sir, I'm, I'm not drunk! I wouldn't do that to your daughter; I mean drive your daughter around drunk," she said imitating his voice and laughing. "Just ignorant. He standing there sweating bullets. He almost didn't let her go."

"For real? Oh my God!" I laughed. "What's up with this necklace he got her?" I wished I were there to see my sisters' boyfriend. It was odd that she was dating now, and I'd give anything to see my dad's reaction to some dude other than him receiving her attention. She was a true daddy's girl.

"Oh God! Don't even get me started on that again. It was some cheap little diamond chip..." Mama started laughing again. "A diamond chip ring he probably got from Wal-Mart. She walking around here showing it off like it's something spectacular. I'm like girl if you don't go sit your tail down somewhere. I don't know where she meets these characters." I could picture her facial expression as she made her latter statement.

"How old is the boy?" I inquired.

"I think she said he nineteen about to be twenty. He isn't in school or anything."

"He got a job at least don't he?" I asked out of curiosity.

"He works at some fast food chain. That wasn't the first time your daddy met him," Mama started laughing again.

51

"Ma, what's so funny?" I asked wanting to be in on the joke as well.

"I guess he came to the house one day when I wasn't home. I'm assuming he had just got off work or something." She started laughing again. "Your daddy said the boy smelled like day old hot dog water," she said bursting into laughter.

"Mama, ya'll so silly," I said laughing.

"Wheeew! So I don't know how serious she is with this boy, but she'd better get her head in the game with school I know that much," my mother said with warning.

"So her grades are slipping?" This was unlike Jasmine. School always came first, so if she was letting her grades fall to the wayside, then she was definitely in some type of love with this guy. They say you get stupid when it happens.

"Yeah, she just ain't been doing what she needs to do. You better talk to her. I'm going to send her to live with you in a minute," she threatened. I knew she was playing, but there was seriousness in her tone as she voiced her concern.

"I'll talk to her tonight," I said trying to reassure her. "You talked to your aunt?"

"Yeah, she wants me to come down and visit with everybody for Thanksgiving." I hadn't seen my cousins on my mom's side in a few years. To know that they were in close proximity to my location was a great discovery. My parents had recently transferred stateside to Texas.

"You gonna go there or come home?"

"I don't know. I told her I was planning on coming home, and that I could come down there sometime before that."

"Oh yeah? How far are you from Columbia?"

"Like three and a half to four hours. It's not too bad. I need to buy a tire for this car though before I put it on the road like that."

"What's wrong with your car?"

"Nothing is wrong with it...it's fine. One of my tires had a slow leak, so they replaced it. But it was low this morning. So I think I might have to replace the rim or something. I don't know."

"Oh well, okay boy, you make sure you doing what you need to be doing. I'll talk to you later."

"Okay, Ma. Love you."

"Bye," she said before hanging up the phone.

After I got off the phone with my mom, I called Shawn to find out if and when they were leaving for Virginia. I got his voicemail, so I left a message and headed over to the gym on base to get a quick workout in.

I entered the gym, which looked like a ghost town surprisingly but then I realized it was Friday and a payday weekend, so kats were not sticking around the base if they could help it. I walked into the aerobic area and began some stretching. I turned up the music in my headphones and started my workout. I did a few sets of crunches and push-ups and decided to do some curls with a dumb bell before getting on the treadmill.

I walked over to the weight room and headed towards the dumbbell stands. I was changing the song with one hand and reaching for a 35lbs weight with the other hand not paying attention to my surroundings when my hand touched the hand of a guy in the gym. We were reaching for the same dumbbell.

"My bad, man. I wasn't paying attention," I said looking up at this gorgeous dark skinned brotha. I recognized him from the clinic. It was the Corpsman who worked at Medical next door. We had been exchanging glances for a while. I didn't think he was gay; however, my gaydar was picking up something when we would lock eyes and speak in passing. I was determined to fish out some details today.

"No, man, it's cool. Hey, um… you work over at Dental, don't you?"

"Yeah, you work at Medical, right?" I said knowing full well I knew the answer to my own question. I removed my head phones, letting them dangle around my neck.

"Yeah, I'm Westbrook, first name is Darius, bruh."

"I'm Williams's man, Jason. Nice meeting you."

"You too. I thought I was the only one off in here and shit."

"I know! It's like a ghost town on payday, huh?" I said smiling. I was trying to read his body language. I was trying to gauge if I should flirt with him or not. I knew I had to be subtle about it though. The only thing on my mind at that point was dumbbells and ding-a-ling. A vision of me spotting him spoke to the desire within me.

"How long are you out here?" I asked watching him readjust the strap on his glove.

"Two years. It's a trip how country it is out here," he said. He wiped his brow with the florescent towel that the gym provided. His muscles flexed and bulged as his palm cupped his forehead. He placed the towel between his gym shorts and the lower portion of his abdomen. The towel dangled from the region of the body where the v-cut separates the legs from the abs. I averted my eyes away from the towel so as not to look conspicuous.

"I know, right? I'm from the Chi, so you know it's a whole new world for me...from the concrete jungle to Green Acres and shit," he said as we both laughed. He was manhandling a water bottle as he squirted water into his mouth. "So, man, where you from?" A drop of water parted ways from his bottom lip.

"I'm from everywhere, dude. I'm an Army brat, but I was born in Detroit, so that's home," I said with a nervous chuckle. In my mind, I was thinking, stop giggling like a little schoolgirl, but everything about this dude right now exuded sex...not just sex but great sex! I tried to snap out of the arousing trance in which I found myself.

"Say word, that's not too far from the crib. It's a

four-hour drive."

"Yeah, I heard. I was trying to get orders to Great Lakes, but they sent me here. So I'll try again the next go round," I said stretching my arms.

"Yeah, that's how they do you, man. Yo' I don't know about going to "Great Mistakes." I want to be away from the crib for a while. My ex-girl is on some ol' other shit, so it's whatever right now," he said slapping the air with his free hand.

"Oh yeah?" I replied with disappointment. My smile faded slightly. I was hoping I didn't roll my eyes.

"Yeah, but yo' bruh, I'ma let you get your lift on and shit. Get at me before you dip out. Maybe we can kick it sometime. Cool?" he said tapping my chest. My dick jumped a little.

"Yeah man, that's cool," I said thinking about him just touching me. I wanted more than that little love tap to happen.

"Cool, I don't meet too many kats from the Midwest," he said winking at me.

"Alright," I said concentrating on controlling an erection.

"A'ight be sure to holler at me before you leave."

I nodded my head in agreement, grabbed a 35lbs dumbbell and walked back to the Aerobic room. Dude was giving me mixed signals. I mean...we had been playing laser tag with our eyes for a few weeks now, and then he tells me about his girl back home. I chocked it up as a loss. I guess it wouldn't hurt to have a straight friend. Hell, he was very nice to look at.

I finished off my workout with a two mile run on the treadmill. I was pumped and mentally preparing for the party scene. I went to stretch and walked into the restroom to wash my hands and wash off the excess sweat from my face, neck and arms. I noticed Darius digging around in a gym bag as I walked out of the restroom. I walked over to him.

"Alright man, I'm about to head out," I said trying to control the size of my smile.

"Cool. Man, I still have a few more sets, but uh, yeah, definitely man, let me give you my number. Get a network going out in this bitch," he smiled.

"Okay, but my phone is in the car," I said. I mentally kicked myself in the butt for leaving my phone in the car of all days, but I make it a habit of not bringing it into the gym.

"Cool, well, I will just put your number in my phone and call yours."

"Okay." I recited my number to him. I looked at his phone to make sure he entered the correct digits.

"A'ight, bet! It's gonna be a 312 number, so get at me. You take it light," he winked.

"Alright man, take care," I said as he dapped me up. His grip sent me into a little frenzy. I definitely had to get out of there, before the obvious happened...

I walked out of the gym to my car and popped the trunk. I grabbed a towel, shut the trunk, and walked over to the driver side. I opened the door, and placed the towel over the seat of the car. I got in and grabbed my phone to check my messages. I had two missed calls from Shawn. I hit talk to return his call. I put my earpiece in and started to head out of the parking lot.

"Hey whore! What's up?" he said. I heard music in the background.

"Hey," I laughed. "Are ya'll still going?" I asked.

"Of course! The club is going to be cute tonight. DJ Sedrik is back in town. We gon' get life!" he said. I heard him snapping his fingers.

"Okay, well I'm just leaving the gym now. So what time are we going to go?" I asked gearing my mind up for the next adventure.

"Um, you can take your time. I am gonna go to the mall, and see about grabbing an outfit and we can meet up around say seven-ish I guess...maybe earlier. It doesn't matter. We usually leave here around 8 and are at the club by midnight. So we'll play it by ear," Shawn said. I felt like he was going to keep pushing the time back. I was anxious to get on the road and experience the gay nightlife, not to mention play with some boys.

"Okay. Should I follow ya'll in my car or what?" I asked thinking maybe I should drive myself in case I needed to escape.

"I was going to drive, so you can ride with us. You can stay with me at my mom's house, and we'll drop Lyzell off at his momma's house after the club."

"Okay, what should I wear?" Switching my mind into how I should look.

"Chile, it's casual, so just your normal gear. I know you have some fierce garments to wear, so no excuses," he said laughing.

"Yeah, I have a few things to wear." I had never worn any of my clothes to a club. On TV shows, they always showed people dressed up, but those were straight folks, on straights shows, at straight establishments. It was like that in real life. Were the rules different at the gay club?

"Oh, and bring something for church. We gotta go to the temple on Sunday. Mrs. Winifred Banks will not hear of us clubbing all night Friday and Saturday and not giving God his glory on the Sabbath," he instructed.

"Alright! Well, I will go get showered and packed. I will hit you up when I'm ready."

"Okay, I will come pick you up let's say 7:30ish that way we can swing by and get that big queen, and be on the road by eight. Alright?"

"Okay Shawn, see ya'll later."

"Bye."

Trade, Faggots, and Stunt Queens

I wasn't really nervous until we crossed the Virginia state line. My mind started to race again thinking about what the club would present. I wondered if it was like what you'd see on TV? Or the episodes of Queer as Folk I'd watched with Shawn and them. I was a fidgety ball of anxious energy all of a sudden. It was a little past midnight, and Shawn reached behind his seat to grab Lyzell's leg to wake him up. He had fallen asleep about an hour and a half into the trip. We took Highway 17 all the way to the Chesapeake, Norfolk, and Portsmouth area of Virginia Beach. It did indeed take just about four hours to get there. Shawn and I talked about all kinds of things, laughed, and pretended to be backup singers for the various musical artists we played.

"Chile, this wave cap is giving me the business! I think I tied it too tight girl." Lyzell said stretching and yawning in the back seat.

"Put your face on girl. We're almost there!" Shawn said.

"Oh we gon' cut up girl! Yes, ma'am honey!" Lyzell said. "Let me fix my French roll girl," he said jokingly. "You got a brush up there?" he asked. Shawn reached into the door pocket, retrieved a brush and handed it to him. I laughed and looked back in the rearview mirror to see if he was putting a wig on or something.

We arrived at the club and parked the car. There was a slight chill in the air. I could hear the bumping of bass from the building in front of us. As we walked through the parking lot, Lyzell and Shawn hugged and greeted various people. They introduced me to a few of them. Lyzell told me that the ones they introduced me to were cool, but the others were late, tired and not worth my time. He would whisper things like, "Look at this stunt queen girl. You know she stole them garments," then turn to them and say, "Heeey! Bitch you look fierce!" It was the funniest thing and so very contrived.

I asked him what a stunt queen was. He explained to me in his own way that they were the girls, girls meaning boys, who would steal your social security number, credit cards, write stolen checks, steal clothes, shoes, groceries, and steal your man when you weren't looking. When he found out that I had my wallet on me, he immediately turned me around so that we could leave it secured in the car.

"Chile, these bitches will hug you and they'll have one of their coverts walk past and reach in them pockets. You can't trust most of these sissies Jason. Just a little FYI." he warned. I took what he said to heart and filed the statements under Street Smarts 101 in my mind.

As we walked towards the building, I spotted a few very attractive men out in the parking lot leaning on their cars. Several other kats were in their cars with the windows down halfway, playing the latest jam, talking, and observing the sights.

This was my first time at a gay club. It was called Nutty Buddy's. How fitting. We made it to the entrance of the club where we were frisked, and then greeted by a drag queen. She was a tall white cross dresser with a red wig done up in two ponytails. Her makeup looked halfway done or like she just began trying it out. It was coated too thick. It looked like she was trying to impersonate a cross between Rainbow Brite and Punky Brewster. I showed my ID and paid my $8.00 to get in.

"Don't be nervous sweetie. I don't bite. Is this your first time?" She said tying a wristband on me.

"Is it that obvious?" I said feigning a smile. I looked over at Shawn who was bopping to the muted sound of the music coming from the other side of the door.

"Honey, it's written all over that sweet little face of yours," she said giving me a wink. I nodded, and let out a nervous giggle as Shawn and Lyzell walked up and paid.

We all walked through the next door out of the foyer, and entered the main party area. They had just started playing house music. DJ Sedrik was on the ones and two's and ever so often you would hear him yell into the microphone "WORK CHILDREN!" or "AAAAH SHIT NOW, THE LEGENDARY HOUSE MOTHER CHANEL OVAH JUST STEPPED IN THE MUTHAFUCKIN' ROOM! DON'T HURT EM SUGAH!"

Being the newbie that I was, I asked Shawn what was a "house." A lot of times, there are drag queens or just older gays in general that take on the role of parents or guardians to gay youth that run away from home or have been kicked out. They form pseudo families   and include their friends within these groups. They are known in the gay scene as House Children. There were various well-known houses, for example the House of Versace, the House of Chanel, the House of Shade, etc. In essence, one could call them a gay fraternity, gang, click; however, you wanted to label it. They would compete in what's known as the ballroom scene. The balls consist of dance battles, vogue routines, or runway type walk-offs of various clothing and modeling categories. This was just something to keep the "kids" off the street and give them a sense of belonging...

The music was pumping so hard; I could feel the bass vibrating in my chest. It felt as if it was circling my heart assisting it to beat. The lights were bright and flashing and the patrons of the club were really partying. The dance floor was packed, and there were also people lining the bar, talking, drinking, smoking, or just leaning back sizing everyone up who walked by.

I saw all types of men there: skinny, tall, heavyset, feminine, masculine, light skinned, dark skinned, Latinos, Blatinos, mixed with a couple of white boys. Kats were rocking everything from Timbs, hoodies, fitted caps, doo- rags, baggy jeans and tees with bling-bling, to wigs, high heels, stockings, skirts, purses and ponytails. The scene looked like a snapshot of Source magazine's 1997 article entitled, "Homo's in Hip-Hop."

We made a tour of the club so I could get a feel for the place. It wasn't too big and it wasn't too small. The second level was a space housing a couple of pool tables, a semi plush lounge area, and a balcony overlooking the dance floor. I noticed a huge mirror outlining two corners of the dance floor. There were people standing in front of it, looking at themselves dance, and a few were coupled up grinding as if they were having sex in the mirror. The energy was intense. I was taking everything in and even got my dance on after I loosened up. I finally knew what it felt like to be free, gay, and happy like the song said. I just let go of all of my inhibitions. I felt safe and able to party without pretending to be something I wasn't. I was having so much fun that I lost track of time. When the song "Percolator" came on, I was getting freaked from behind and freaking some cutie in front of me. The feeling of having two warm male bodies pressed against my own was wonderful. I didn't want the night to end. Shawn came over towards the end of the song smiling in my face. He said it was the last song. We finished dancing, and I noticed I was soaked with sweat. The guy dancing behind me hugged me and whispered his name in my ear. I think he said his name was Darnell. It was too much going on to remember. He told me he'd see me around as I followed Shawn toward the exit. We walked outside, and made our way to the car.

The cool night air hit me like a ton of bricks as we carried our sweat drenched bodies through the exit.

Folk were laughing and joking with one another. Some were hugged up with each other, or posted up trying to get attention from those walking by.

"Okay, chile, did you get life?" Shawn asked.

"Yes, I had a good time. It was fun," I said.

"Well good! That boy you were dancing with was cute. I was like ALRIGHT! Work whore!" Lyzell said laughing.

"Okay! He was a cutie. I don't think I've seen him in there before," Shawn recalled. I laughed along with them blushing at the same time.

"So you guys come here all the time?" I asked.

"Yes, ma'am! Every chance we get to break away from Lejeune honey!" Lyzell screeched as he broke out into a dance. "I'm feeling my cocktail girls. Now all I need is a cock in my tail, honey! Go warm the car up girl. I'ma go chat these dates honey!"

"Chile, that queen is a mess. We're gonna trail the kids to Granby Street. That's where everyone goes to hangout after the club to parking lot pimp," Shawn said.

"Okay. Sounds like a plan," I said observing our surroundings. I was still intoxicated with the feeling I had inside the club. I was on cloud nine. I can't remember being this loose and at ease. I was around my own kind. YES!!!

"Hopefully Alice won't cut up tonight like she did last time," Shawn said.

"Alice? Who is Alice?" I asked puzzled.

"Oh, my bad! That's code for the police. We say

"Alice" or "Vera," Shawn said laughing. "That bitch is EVIL round these here parts." We high-fived each other.

"Okay, I guess," I said cracking up laughing. Ya'll know ya'll have some terms. I shook my head.

Give it time, and you will be kee-keeing and cutting up with the phrases too," Shawn said patting my shoulder.

We walked to the car and posted up for a few minutes waiting on Lyzell. Shawn and I were talking with some of his friends. We were listening to the music coming from the car and just acting silly. Lyzell came by and hugged everyone. We noticed people starting to drive out of the parking lot. We got in the car and started to follow the caravan of cars towards the infamous Granby Street in Norfolk. We had the music blasting from the speakers, and I had a broad smile on my face laughing at the antics of Shawn and Lyzell. The night air kept the feeling of freedom alive. If this was what getting your life was, I tell you, I was getting it. We sped along the strip as the two of them were waving and shouting to the other guys driving in the collective group. We made it to Granby Street and parked in an empty lot with a huge Maytag mural painted on the side of one of the adjacent buildings. More and more cars started rolling in, and bodies started flooding the lot walking around, chatting it up, and just having a good time. The parking lot looked like the club in a sense. People were dancing, hugged up, kissing, and acting as if nothing else on Earth mattered. For this to be the

South, it was amazing how many kats were out being gay. I was in awe! There were so many variations of masculinity. Seeing it on TV is one thing, having a general idea in your head can't compare, but seeing it in person is jaw dropping. Just because a boy looked like a boy didn't mean he was straight, and   I quickly observed that a fitted cap didn't make you a man. I was starting to see and learn the differences between "tops" and "bottoms," a seemingly taboo and at times, touchy subject within the community. I was all smiles, leaning against Shawn's car as the guy I was dancing with made his way over to me. He clocked me, "You a Navy boy, huh?" I laughed and confirmed his assumption. We engaged in conversation and exchanged numbers. Soon after, the police rolled around to break up the night's events and sent everyone home. The night's fun had officially come to a close, but what a night it was to remember...

After we left Granby Street, Shawn dropped Lyzell off at his mother's house, and we headed back to his parents' house. It was just past five in the morning on Sunday, and I was pretty sleepy. We pulled into the driveway, and quietly made our way into the house to finally get some much needed rest. I walked into the guest bedroom and took off my shoes, shirt, and socks, and laid down in the bed. I remember getting very comfortable and it felt as if I were only sleep for five minutes. I thought I was dreaming, until I heard my name being called. I could feel someone gently rubbing my shoulder. I rolled over and opened my eyes to the sight of Shawn's mother, an older woman, short in stature that I recognized from picture's Shawn has shown me. She seemed to be sweet and had the demeanor of a "Southern Belle," but all I could think about was what the hell does she want at this time of morning?!?!?!?!?!

"Jason," she said as I wondered how she knew my name. Apparently, Shawn had told her all about me. "Hi, sweetie! It's a pleasure to meet you. I know you all were out all night having fun, but you need to get up soon for church darling. We will be leaving for the temple at nine- sharp. You can ride with Shawny. Now when you take your shower, don't stay in there too long, baby. If you run the water too long, the water bill gonna be sky high," she warned.

Church! I yelped inside my head, but answered with a sleepy, "Okay, I won't," as I rubbed my eyes mad as hell that this woman has disturbed my rest!

"You can lie here for a little bit longer, or you can come to morning service. I'll let you decide. You want to come to morning service?"

"No, I want to sleep for like five more minutes, ma'am. I promise I'll be ready." I really wanted to say, Lady, will you leave me the hell alone!?!?!?

"Okay darling. Don't doze off too hard now," she said.

"Okay, I won't," I said still irritated. I pulled the cover over my head. I started to get comfortable again, but I was soon startled by the sound of singing coming from the family room. I opened my eyes wide and realized that the vocalists were Shawn, his mother, and his father. His mother was leading as Shawn and his father sang background. I placed my hand over my mouth as my ears perked up to hear the sounds of the Banks family serenading Jesus.

"THIS MORNING WHEN I ROSE, YEAH!" Shawn's mother sang.

"I DIDN'T HAVE   NO DOUBT!" a male singing voice followed that I later learned was his father.

"OOOOOOH, THIS MORNING WHEN I ROOOOOSE, YEEES! she sang louder.

"I DIDN'T HAVE NO DOUBT!" he responded.

I felt like I was in the twilight zone! What the hell! I realized that with this call and response going on, it would be best to just go ahead and get the hell up. I laughed to myself thinking, Well, she tried to warn me. I made an urgent mental note to talk about Shawn later; this was hilarious. I knew he was a church boy, but DAMN! Service at home before service. I mean I grew up in the church too, but to me, this was quite a bit much.

I got out of the bed put on a t-shirt, quickly washed my face, and brushed my teeth. I walked into the family room during the middle of the second song of the morning.

"PUT YOUR MIND ON JESUS!" Shawn's mother sang.

"Praise his name!" Shawn and his father responded.

"PUT YOUR MIND ON JESUS!"

"He's alright!"

I joined in. I figured when in the country, do as the locals do.

You've Got Game

My first gay club experience was just the tip of the iceberg of experiencing all things gay. After that night, my life changed, and I became more and more comfortable with me and my friends. Michael, Shawn, and Preston were a welcomed addition to my life. I was dating other guys and even spending more time with gym rat Darius. We had become workout partners and helped one another study for the advancement exam. One could almost call him a closet case, but in talking with him, I learned that he was on a journey of self-discovery the same as me.

One day during the end of a three-mile run, he asked what I was doing for the upcoming Labor Day weekend. I told him I was going to Atlanta. I didn't have to mention that I was going for Pride, he already knew and exclaimed in disbelief, "for the gay shit?" I guess my laughter confirmed his suspicions and from there a bond and a myriad of questions ensued. It was the start of "his gay shit" hitting the fan...

Just when I thought things couldn't get any better than Nutty Buddy's and Granby Street, Michael, Shawn, Preston, and I went to Atlanta, GA – the black gay mecca of the South, where I had my Pride cherry popped, and I became an official card carrying member of the gay community. I swore I heard a round of applause from the heavens. It was an experience to end all experiences and the beginning for me...

73

I never knew so many gay men existed until I went to Atlanta's pride. From the time, we got there all we saw were men, men, men, and more men, especially in the host hotel in downtown Atlanta, where we stayed. All weekend long, we traipsed through the city in our rented SUV going from club to club to club, and event to event to event. We laughed and joked the whole time, but it was about half-way through the trip that I began to have the most fun...

I don't quite recall if it was Saturday or Sunday night because we were all over the city, but whatever day it was, we were in chill mode. We'd made it to Club 708, which was the hotspot of the night. There was a massive line, and they were replacing those coming out of the club with a fresh face from those patiently waiting. The parking lot proved to be a strong rival to the club. There were so many phyne muthafuckas out. It was like something out of a movie or a fantasy come to life. Atlanta seemed like the deal, and if you were a black gay man, this was where you needed to be. Michael and Preston went to try their luck at getting into the club. Shawn and I stayed behind. We opened the tailgate put on some music; kee kee'd, and chatted with some of the guys passing by who stopped to talk with us.

Shawn eventually went to find somewhere to use the restroom. I sat on the tailgate of the SUV drinking a Snapple. I was in my own little world for a minute when I felt the truck rock a little bit. I turned to my left and observed this tall caramel complexioned brotha leaning up against the truck. He flashed me the sexiest smile I had seen all weekend. He was gripping a Corona with his left hand and resting against the truck on his right arm. He was wearing a Boston Celtics Jersey revealing a very nice set of well-defined arms, and a nice sculpted chest. He had on a baggy pair of jean shorts showing off his toned calf muscles, and a fresh pair of crisp white Air Force One's. He also rocked short length dreads that stopped just at the nape of his neck. They were neatly pulled back. I broke out of my trance, smiled back, and played it cool wondering what line he was going to throw.

"You need a ride or something?" I asked as I took a sip of my drink.

"Nope! I gotta whip. I could use your help on the passenger side though," The stranger said rather confidently.

"Is that right?" I asked trying not to laugh.

"That's right," he said looking sexy as hell.

"So you must run like, a cab service using lines like that? Does that one work much for you?" I asked sarcastically. He laughed a little bit still holding his ground. He took a long swig of beer.

"I like that in you. You got jokes, but naw, just cause I rock my dreads don't mean I'm a Cabby. Plus, it made you laugh, so it worked, right?" he said.

"How about stepping to me with your name, dread man?" I said smiling. He stopped leaning on the truck.

He was still flashing that beautiful smile of his when he extended his right hand out toward me.

"I'm Gary. What's your name?" he inquired. I looked down at his hand and then squarely into his eyes.

"Is that your real name?" I asked with a smirk.

"That's my real name sexy, so what's up?" he said with his hand still extended. "I'm Gary."

"I'm Jason," I said smiling. I shook his hand. He gripped it tightly and allowed the handshake to linger for a second as if he were taking in my energy. It turned me on, just as much as the intensity of his eyes. I bit my bottom lip and offered him the green light with a flirtatious glare.

"Nice to finally meet you, Jason. I thought you were going to leave ya' man hangin," he said smiling again.

"You as well. My bad," I said with a slight laugh. I took another sip of my Snapple.

"You mind if I chill here with you for a minute? I mean your dude ain't gon' be rolling up on me or no shit like that right?" he said as he took another gulp of beer. I stretched my arm out motioning for him to take a seat. He sat on the bumper.

"So, you come to these Pride things often?" Gary asked. I laughed.

"Dang! We really need to update your game," I said trying not to laugh too hard.

"Aww, how you gon' bust me out like that?" he said trying to conceal the slight embarrassment he felt. "I feel you though. I'ma be real with you Jason, I'm out of practice," he laughed. I loved the way my name rolled off of his tongue. "But I've seen you around a couple of times this weekend and told myself if I saw you again before I left I would get at you," Gary said with a boyish smile on his face at that point.

"Aww, my first real stalker...that's hot! Where did you see me?" I said smiling at him. I was trying to figure out if I had seen him around, but his face was not familiar to me.

"Naw, nothing like that. I just go after what I want. I guess I'm losing my cool a little bit. You're a sexy lil' nigga, for real! So forgive me if I'm a bit lame right about now," he said laughing at himself.

"You're pretty sexy yourself man. You're rocking the hell out of that jersey. Plus, your smile kept my attention." I noticed how pretty his teeth were. I guess that was a curse of my profession. I like kissing, so I always notice a nice set of lips and teeth on a dude.

"That's what I'm talking about. And I think I saw you at the hotel. You staying at the Sheridan right?" he asked. "Yeah, with my boys," I said trying to figure out how I could have missed seeing him but he's seen me numerous times. "This is my first Pride."

"You enjoying yourself?" he asked. He winked at me this time.

"Dude, I'm having a ball out here! This is so cool, all these phyne dudes and then I'm with my boys cutting the fool," I said looking around. I looked over in his direction. "Who you here with? You can't possibly be by yourself?" I asked out of curiosity. He seemed to give me that playboy vibe.

"I'm out here with my boy Andre this go round, gettin it in before I head back home." He paused and took a sip of beer. "Looking for my next victim," he said with a devilish grin.

"Is that right?" I replied. I was wondering if my suspicions were right.

"That's right, sexy."

"I see, so where is home?" I asked, moving the conversation along.

"Chi-town baby!"

"Oh, for real?" I said with excitement. "I've always wanted to go up there. I'm from Detroit originally, but me and a couple of my boys are planning to make Chicago the next big move."

"Word?"

"Yup," I said thinking maybe I was revealing a bit too much too soon.

"I think you'll like it up there. It's a ton of shit to do year round, even in the dead of winter. Plus, I'm there, so you know, it's live," he said popping his collar.

"Oh yeah? Well, I plan on checking it out soon," I said.

"I could take you on a little tour or something, show you the ropes and shit," he said as Shawn and Preston walked up. Shawn was giving me the side eye glance as he observed the situation.

"So I see someone is making friends," Preston said smiling. He clasped his hands together and gave Gary a once over.

"Gary, these are a couple of my boys, Shawn and Preston," I said pointing at them respectively. "Shawn and Preston this is Gary."

"Nice to meet you, fellas," Gary said shaking their hands individually.

"Did ya'll get into the club?" I asked.

"Mike is still in there copping booty feels and getting numbers. It's too much going on in there, chile. I couldn't breathe. Hell, the club is out here," Preston said as we all laughed.

"Well, if you gentleman don't mind, I'd like to steal your boy Jason for a little while longer if it's cool with him," he interrupted looking at Shawn and Preston, then at me. "Can you walk and talk with me?" He caught me off guard with his request. I tried not to blush but maintain my composure.

"Alright now," Shawn said looking at Preston. They both smiled and turned towards me awaiting my response.

"It's cool, I can walk with you for a minute," I said standing up. I adjusted the tank top I was wearing and stood next to him before we made our exit.

"Alright, fellas, I promise to be good. I'll bring him back safe and in one piece." Gary assured them. "Nice meeting the two of you!"

"It was nice meeting you, Gary," Shawn said as he

grabbed my arm. "You'd better work, bitch. Damn he phyne!" he spoke in my ear in a hushed tone. I mouthed a quick, okay! before turning to Preston.

"See you in a bit, sweetie," Preston said as we walked away. I waved to the two of them.

"I'm not ready to lose your attention yet," Gary said once again flashing me that smile. He placed his hand on the small of my back guiding me next to him. I smiled back as my back relaxed against his firm grip.

"I see. So what type of victim am I?" I asked still smiling. I looked up at him and caught his eye. He laughed.

"Aww man! I did say I was on the prowl, huh?" he laughed.

"Uh yeah, pretty much. I mean as enticing as you are, I'm not that dude. Just for clarification," I said folding my arms.

"You're a feisty one, aren't you? I like that in you," he said nodding his head. We walked at a leisurely pace oblivious to the rest of the activity surrounding us.

"I mean...I just like to be up front." I winked.

"I respect that. Now you really got my attention. As you can see, it's plenty of ass around here for the taking, and yours is quite lovely," he said checking out my butt, "but seeing you around, and then talking to you so far, it's something about you I like. So you could be the next Mr. Larrieux. Who knows?" he said shrugging his shoulders.

"Yeah maybe, depending on if the stars align in your

favor," I said with a smirk. I finished the last of my drink and recapped the bottle.

"Cool! So now that we got all of that out of the way. Tell me a little bit about Jason."

"Like what?" I asked wanting him to be less vague in his questioning.

"What do you do? Some of your likes, dislikes. You know the basics. Lay the foundation for me and we'll build from there," Gary said as we made our way around a group of guys dancing.

"Well, I am currently in the Navy," I said proudly.

"Word?" he said giving me a hand salute. I laughed.

"So what do you do for the Navy?"

"I work as a Dental Assistant for now. I want to ultimately be a Dental Hygienist." I paused as he nodded and then asked, "And what do you do besides look for victims?" I said gesturing the quotation sign.

"Oh, I'm a porn star. You might have seen me in a few Enrique Cruz movies," he said with a straight face.

My face instantaneously contorted as to suggest that I didn't like that answer at all. "Oh. Well...okay." I said not knowing how to respond. In my head, I was thinking. ABORT! ABORT! ABORT!

"I'm fucking with you Jason," he said bursting into laugher and ribbing me.

"Oh! Boy, you so silly. I was like, wow! I mean, if that's what you do, then, hey," I said embarrassed for falling for his comment.

"I'm a Fire Fighter. Truthfully," he said letting out a

laugh. "I've been doing that for five and a half years, and I really enjoy it."

"Okay, that's hot! So you're a hero and stuff? What made you want to become a Fireman?"

Well, my Dad really. My family is from the Bahamas. I was born there, and my folks moved the family to the States in the early 80's. That was what my Pops wanted to be, so I followed in his footsteps. He used to take me to the station with him and I would play on the fire trucks and slide down the pole."

"Aww! How cute. So you and your Dad are close." I thought that was a great quality. It reminded me of how my Dad and I used to work on cars together when I was younger.

"Yeah, we have our moments like any other father and son, but firefighting keeps us close."

"Cool. I wish I could say the same thing about me and my Dad."

"Do you guys talk at all?"

"It's complicated. Maybe I'll tell you about it one day," I said not wanting to get to heavy with the conversation just yet.

"I'll be all ears. So how do you occupy your time when you're not preparing for war or fixing teeth?" he said lightening the mood.

"It all depends. I pretty much do what comes to mind. I love going to movies, being outdoors, my Dad and I share a love for cars, exercise, I do a lot of writing, and love cooking when I get the chance."

"Oh word, you cook?" he said rubbing his stomach.

"Yeah, I love to cook. I don't get to do it that often because I live in the barracks at the moment." I thought to myself how cool it would be to whip up something for him.

"What's your specialty?"

"I make an awesome Manicotti dish." I confidently stated. "I love Italian food. I have a Chicken Cordon Bleu recipe that I want to try one day."

"Oh shit, you got to look me up when you come to Chicago. I have a large kitchen with everything you need to make me a meal." he said nodding his head like a little kid.

"You crazy. So you don't cook?" I asked.

"Nope. Now I can grill up some stuff, but straight up cooking? Nope. I need my future boyfriend for that." He winked.

"I see. So is that what you're looking for? A boyfriend?" I asked.

"Yes. As I get older I would like to find someone worthwhile to be with. I'll be twenty-nine in November. How old are you by the way?"

"I'll be twenty-two in January."

"Oh you a lil' young'un," he said. He started rubbing his hands together.

"I guess so, but I got my act together to be twenty-one," I stated as a matter of fact.

"I see that," he said checking out my butt again. I laughed at him. "So what do you want? What are you looking for?"

"I'm a young dude. Who knows what I want. The idea of being in a relationship is cool. I haven't really had my feelings hurt yet, but I think ultimately I want a dude I can one day go to church with."

"I heard that. Well, come to Chicago, so I can make up your mind."

"How are you going to do that?"

"Come to my city. And I got you," he said sizing me up. He stopped and we sat on a brick fence at the end of the parking lot.

"I don't know about all that," I said trying to play hard to get.

"...Which is why you need me. I'll make your mind up in that department," he said ribbing me once more. I looked at him from the corner of my eye. I reached into my pocket and handed him my phone. He looked down at my hand and continued, "Oh, so you're trying to exchange numbers?" He winked at me taking the phone in his hand.

We continued a smooth initial getting to know you type of interview with one another as he punched his number into my phone. I didn't want to reveal too much of myself too soon, and I hoped that he was taking an interest in me. To my surprise, he asked if he could steal me away from my friends the next day. I agreed thinking, "Why not?" Little did I know he would steal more than just my time; he would eventually steal my heart...

Our chat came to a close when Michael called to let me know that the crew was ready to leave. I gave Gary a warm lingering hug. His warmth and the scent of his invigorating cologne gave me something to dream about that night. When we released one another I smiled and walked away. I turned around and he was smiling watching me. I laughed recalling Loretta Devine's scene in Waiting to Exhale. I rushed back to the fellas anticipating answering a million questions...

"So don't be giving this nigga no ass, Jay! You keep them panties around your waist not your ankles," Michael said. He was holding my arm and acting as if I were his child and he was my father.

"Boy, If you don't get off of me. You're going to wrinkle my shirt up hag!" I replied.

"I'm not playing Jason. Remember everyone has HIV until tested negative," Michael said gradually loosening his grip. We were having our own side bar conversation in the adjoining room while everyone was busy getting ready for more pride festivities.

"Calm it on down hag!" I said. "Did you screw that old man from the other night?" I questioned.

"Which one?" Michael asked smiling. I already knew the answer. Michael had a veracious appetite for sex and since I was still fairly green behind the ears when it came to certain things, sex was a topic that I addressed with him on occasion just to obtain a little knowledge. Hearing about his conquests was always entertaining and left me living vicariously in the world of gay sex.

"Which one?" I said with a hint of sarcasm. "Michael, you know which one don't play dumb," I said as he and I chuckled.

"I tore that ass up, Jay. Oooh that booty was good!!!!" he said humping the air.

"I am so mad you had sex with somebody's Grandpa," I laughed.

"I know right, but Grandparents can get this dick too," he said placing his arm around my shoulders.

"He didn't look fifty though. He looked good for his age. They say black don't crack," I said folding my arms.

"He wants me to hit it again before we leave," Michael added.

"You gon' do it?" I asked trying not to laugh.

"I might hit it tonight. I'm supposed to be meeting these other two guys for a threesome later. That's why these ho's need to HURRY UP GETTING READY! I got a lot of ass to get before we leave in the morning." Michael said looking at his watch. "Shit! Jason it ain't enough time for all this ass I need."

"You are such a whore," I said. Michael definitely had a way with the fellas. I mean the boy could talk your Daddy out of his draws if given a chance. Even I had to admit, there is something about them Georgia boys. If we had of met under any other pretenses, I'd probably be a notch on Michael's bedpost.

"You just don't become one. Don't trade places, you hear me?"

"I know boy, ain't nothing going down until I'm ready for it," I said.

"Resist temptation tonight with that man, Jay, don't let him pressure you. You don't know what he got." Michael warned. I said goodbye to everyone and made my way downstairs to the main lobby to meet Gary for our date. He had convinced me to spend the day with him. I kept what Michael told me in the back of my mind. Before we came out here he had confided in me that he was HIV positive the same day I told him I was a virgin and sort of scared to have sex.

So far I was the only one in the group who knew, and I promised him I would keep it between him and me until he was ready to forego his own big reveal. We had really grown close in the short time we had known each other. We both wanted to move to Chicago to evolve and create new chapters in our lives.

Michael told me he became positive after the first guy he had sex with infected him. He was diagnosed three days after his 20th birthday. He was now twenty-four. The guy was his first real boyfriend who he had fallen in love with and he never questioned the use of condoms. He told me how much he had trusted the guy and how devastated he was thinking that his hopes, dreams, and military career would be over. He told his parents, whom to his surprise, were very supportive. They helped him deal with his situation through lots of prayer, fasting, and simply being there for their son.

I could see the hurt as he told me his story. When he confronted the guy with his results, the guy shrugged it off as if Michael just told him he had the common cold. He then accused Michael of trying to forge documents to start an argument and pretend to be sick to trap him into the relationship.

Michael also told me about bug chasers. These are individuals who feel they are going to ultimately get infected with the virus. They deliberately have unprotected sex with known infected individuals to speed up the process. How crazy! I was also amazed to learn that there are bareback sex parties that cater to this group of like minds. He also warned me of guys who have it, know they have it, and don't care who they pass the virus onto. Michael pleaded with me to hold on to my virginity for as long as possible. He wanted me to be extra careful if and when I did decide to have sex with someone. "I don't want to be the one to welcome you into the Pastor's AIDS club," he told me. I took heed to his warning...

The elevator doors opened. I took a deep breath and walked past two lesbians hugged up holding a bag from the Hustler Store. They were waiting to get into the elevator. I walked into the lobby of the hotel and looked around. There were numerous men and women posted throughout the hotel lobby. A few were scantily clad being taken advantage of mentally by peering eyes. I decided to sit down on one of the chairs in an area Gary could see me once he came down. I was walking and playing with my phone when I felt someone tug on my arm.

"So you gonna walk past your man, sexy?" Gary asked standing up.

"Well I didn't see you." I said smiling. I was startled a little and seeing him at that moment brought about a little surge of nervous energy.

He was wearing a black long sleeved collar shirt, buttoned halfway revealing a slightly hairy chest, and he had the sleeves rolled up showing off a silver Movado wristwatch. He wore a nice pair of jeans and a really nice pair of black Steve Madden shoes. We complemented each other as I had on a pair of fitted distressed faded black jeans, white leather shoes, and a long sleeve white- collar shirt, tapered to hug my torso. I too had it buttoned down halfway, and wore my sleeves rolled up.

"I know. You were all into that phone of yours."

"You always seem to catch me off guard," I said with a nervous giggle.

"Yeah, I got to keep you on your toes. You're one of them independent bottoms." he stated matter of factly.

"I'm mad you think you know my sexual proclivity." I said smiling.

"I'm very observant. It's my job to know," he said smiling. "So I'm right, huh?"

"You took a stab in the dark actually," I said making a go for the exit.

"Not so fast, shorty. I got to wrap my arms around that body first," he said pulling me into him. His mannish nature turned me on so much, not to mention the smell of his cologne.

"You smell good? What is the name of your cologne?" I asked as he released me.

"Bvalgari. You heard of it?"

"No, I'm not really into fragrances. My Pops used to douse me in Polo before church when I was a kid. I feel like I can't breathe when I wear that stuff," I remembered, "but on you it's great," I complimented.

"You smell pretty good yourself though, is that body oil?"

"Nope, just a good quality lotion," I laughed. I was a little nervous, and I was hoping he couldn't tell. I wanted to act like I wasn't fazed by his presence.

"Well, come on let's make brunch happen and enjoy the rest of the day together. Daddy hungry!" he said winking at me and rubbing his stomach.

He placed his hand on the small of my back as he did the other night and led me out of the hotel. He handed a ticket to the valet and a few minutes later the attendant pulled up in an Eddie Bauer Expedition. Gary tipped the driver and opened the door for me to get in. He smiled at me as he walked to the driver side of the SUV.

"So listen, I think it would be nice to take a break from this gay scene, so I'm going to take you to this really nice Bed and Breakfast in Duluth for brunch. We can eat and then walk around the property a little bit, find a spot, and just soak in each other's energy. Cool?" he said smiling.

"That sounds cool to me. I'm in a chill sort of mood. I've been going and going. You know?" I said fastening my seatbelt.

"I feel you. Same here. I'm surprised you were willing to break away from your crew. I'm almost a complete stranger, you know?"

"I can defend myself," I said putting up my fists in a

karate pose.

"Oh okay, but I could fold your little butt up into my pocket."

"Whatever. Don't under estimate my stature," I laughed shaking my head.

"I won't. I like 'em sexy, slim, and petite. He gave me a head nod. How tall are you?" he asked.

"I'm 5'7," and 155," I said wanting to be wrapped up in another one of his tight hugs.

"Ummm! That's what I'm talking about. I love your size. That's perfect."

"Don't love it yet. This is still the interview stage. I need to get my Montel Williams on," I said smiling, trying to play hard ball.

"Oh you'll like it. Trust me. I got this," he said winking at me.

"You so silly! I realized just how that sounded," I said. He laughed.

"Out of the abundance of the heart, the mouth speaks," he said glancing over at me.

"I know right. So like, what are your stats?" I asked sizing him up.

"I'm 6'1" ...around 200."

"That's hot!" I smiled.

"Ah, see you liking that shit, huh?" he asked ribbing me.

"I mean, yeah. I like dudes bigger and taller than me. It's a turn on, like your cologne," I said moving closer to him to inhale the fragrance. I guess I was getting over my nervousness.

"I feel you. How many niggas cologne you been sniffing on out here?" he said with a smirk on his face. I sucked my teeth.

"Nobody's!" I repositioned myself in the seat to get comfortable.

"Now, Jason," he said giving me the side eye.

"I've been swatting dudes away like flies, gassing me up with these tired old, Bobby Womack and Bell Biv Devoe lines."

"What you know about Bobby Womack?" he asked laughing.

"Probably as much as you do," I said coyly.

"What's the worst one you've heard?" he said laughing.

"Yo', I could use some help on the passenger side," I said teasing him about the previous night when we met, trying not to laugh.

"Oh, so you gon' take it there, huh! But where you sitting right now?" he said laughing, tapping my leg.

"It's my pleasure though." I paused momentarily observing just how good looking he was. His eyes were the color of honey and his lips looked like they would feel lovely pressed against my own. I then continued, "That's why I'm here with you," I said flirting again. I bit my lip slightly and let it slide from between my teeth.

"Oh yeah? Thank you for helping me out," he said winking. I laughed.

"Yeah, it's nice and cozy over here," I smiled looking

out of the window. There was a slight moment of silence. Talking to him was pretty easy. There was a nice flow of back and forth flirting with Gary easing over to my side of the truck. He had one hand on the steering wheel and rested his arm on the center console as he continued the conversation.

"You mentioned something about being in Japan the other night...how long were you there?"

"Just a year. It was pretty cool. The Japanese are on a whole other level. Its wild crazy over there," I said with nostalgic resonance.

"Oh yeah? Why you ain't stay?"

"I'm an army brat, so we were stationed over in Germany for a while. And then the Navy sends me back overseas after training. I was just ready to be stateside. I had been overseas my whole time in high school." We stopped at the red light. We made direct eye contact, and it was the first time I had truly noticed how beautiful his eyes were. They were a radiant hazel green.

"Damn, so you are a cultured black man... not a common hood," he said directing his attention away from me when the light changed to green.

"I guess you can say that. I've been to a few places. I'm just blessed man. Have you ever been overseas?" I was anticipating looking deeper into his eyes.

"Nope, just the Bahamas' to visit my family. Nothing special like Europe or Japan. That's pretty sweet. So did you go anywhere else in Europe?" he asked catching me staring at him. He smiled as I answered his question.

"Yeah, I got to see Paris, Spain, the Czech Republic, and Italy."

"That's a beautiful thing," he said. He sounded impressed with my travel resume. "I gotta get out of the country more."

"How is the Bahamas?" I had always been fascinated with the Caribbean culture and the people. It was definitely a place I wanted to visit one day. He really had my attention now.

"Very tropical. It has a few bad areas, but it's very scenic. I love the weather and the way the sun feels on my body. I walk around all day shirtless, getting my tan on, eating, and chillin' at the beach being a bum. Maybe if you stay in my world, I can take you. I think you'll love it. It's laid back like you seem to be."

"Really? I'd like that...if I'm still in your world," I said smiling. I would certainly take him up on his offer when the invitation presented itself.

"Oh yeah?"

"We'll see what happens. You know how ya'll kats do."

"Bet, but I'm not your average," he said.

"I see; so why are you single?" I inquired, "Give me the warning signs," I commanded.

"Aww young'un! If anybody needs to worry, it's me! If I recall correctly, you told me you didn't know what you wanted," he said with a smirk.

"Oh okay! You may have won this round, but there

will be others." I said smiling, as he laughed. "But I'm new to the scene, and dating, and all that yah yah. I was semi- sheltered being an army brat overseas and all. So I'm coming in the game a little late. I don't want to play Charades any more acting as if I'm straight."

"I guess that answer will suffice." He smiled.

"It's the truth, punk," I said lightly punching him in the arm. I rolled my eyes and sucked my teeth.

"Oh, so you got a violent streak huh? Let me add that to the list."

"Whatever man!" I said in a smug tone.

"Seriously, and as you get to know me, you'll see I'm going to always keep it real with you no matter what. I had a really bad break up with my ex Desjardin a few years ago. He was the first dude I fell in love with, and to make a long story short, he broke my heart. It was crazy the way things ended. He just left. Dude just punked out of our situation. No real goodbye, no note, no email, shit, not even some break-up sex. Crazy huh?" he said shaking his head.

"Whoa! I am so sorry to hear that," I said rubbing his arm, which made him muster up a smile.

"It's cool. He was one of my seasons I guess. So I took it in stride." I could tell that he still had an unsettling feeling surrounding the incident.

"How long were you two together?" I asked trying to dig a little deeper.

"Almost three years." he said, giving me a quick glance.

"So what did you do afterwards?" I asked choosing my words carefully.

"Well, I moped around for a few days and slowly got over it. After that I became a ho. My thinking was niggas don't give a damn about me, so I don't give a damn about them. I'm freezing up on that now though. Meaningless sex is not appealing to me now. So it's been a while. I'm putting a hurtin' on the next kat I get with, but I want it to mean something," he said looking at me.

"It's not happening with me during ATL's freak fest," I said laughing.

"Damn!" he said snapping his fingers in a feminine manner. He laughed.

"When was your last time if you don't mind me asking?" I asked bashfully.

"About two months ago. For me, that's a very long time."

"Um huh. I see." I smiled nodding my head.

"Let's change the subject, cause damn. I am not painting a great image in your head right now, am I?"

"It's real though. I value open communication. The real, as you put it," I said still intrigued by him. I could tell he wasn't going to sugarcoat things with me. He was really showing me his human side and opening up.

"Cool. So you've never had a boyfriend or nothing?" he said looking at me sideways.

"Don't look at me like that," I laughed. He laughed too. "I've had crushes on dudes, but messing with kats while I was at the crib was out of the question and then definitely not in boot camp or Japan. So I was ready to get back stateside to do my thing."

"I feel you."

"I was kind of talking to this dude where I'm stationed now."

"Which is where?"

"Camp Lejeune, North Carolina. It's based out of a small town called Jacksonville."

"Okay. So what's up with your boy?" he asked with a little jealousy in his voice.

"Well, I think dude is phyne, but he's one of those confused bisexual dudes. I believe he's gay, but playing the role. I mean we talk all the time and spend time together, but like the closest we've gotten intimately has been cuddling up watching a movie or the occasional peck on the cheek. He's a trip," I stated downplaying and fondly recalling the times I had spent with Darius.

"I know all about the confused brothas. They're all one of God's greatest challenges," he said sarcastically.

"Yeah, but he is so cool, and if anything, a good friendship with him will be cool."

"He in the Navy?"

"Yeah, he is."

"So have you dated anyone else?"

"Yeah, I have," I laughed.

"Sounds like you have a story to tell."

"Oh my God, do I!" I said recalling a disastrous date.

99

"What's up?" he smiled.

"Okay, my boy had hooked me up on Black Planet, I think. And I met this kat who I chit chatted with for a couple of weeks. He asked me out for dinner and a movie. I was like cool. I get over to dude's crib and he invites me in. It looked as if he wasn't ready yet because he was wearing a Nike warm up suit...We talked for a minute, and he offers me a drink. I asked for a bottle of water. He goes to get it and brings it back. Around this same time, my phone is going off. I had an alarm set, and I couldn't get it to stop. So I'm fumbling around with the phone and noticed some activity in my peripheral view. I turn my head in his direction, and this fool has a pacifier in his mouth, has his dick in his hand, jacking off staring at me with this real crazy look."

"Get the fuck out of here!" he said bursting into laughter. I don't believe you!"

"I'm serious! I can't make this stuff up!" I said laughing and holding my hand up as if I were swearing in.

"What did you do?" he said laughing.

"I grabbed my keys and got the hell up out of there. That was some scary stuff man. And the funny thing about it was that dude didn't even move as I was leaving. So I don't know what his deal was. I was like, dude, this isn't for me. It's been real. And he didn't say anything. He just kept jacking off," I said shaking my head and rubbing my eye.

"Oh he was trying to get that nut. Damn, that's

some crazy shit. Have you heard from him at all?"

"No. And he seemed normal on the phone even though I had a strange feeling about meeting him." I laughed picturing him in the chair. "So I think I'm done with the whole internet thing. I've met some cool kats just being out and about."

"Yeah, that Internet man. You never know what the hell you're going to get. You can be anything you want to be, like some In Living Color type shit."

"I know right." I laughed.

"Well, at least you made it out safely."

"I know right." I said, just as we made our way into the parking lot of the restaurant. We walked inside and continued talking. The chemistry was so on point. I was physically and mentally attracted to this dude. I could feel my emotions tying into him. I guess I pictured myself getting wrapped up in someone later in life, but I could get used to having him in my life. I was digging the way he treated me like I was his equal, but at the same time he offered just the right amount of aggression as if to say, "Yo' I got this." My submission seemed to link up to his dominance with the precision of two brand new puzzle pieces being mated.

I felt comfortable talking to him, and he seemed to enjoy my conversation as well. Over dinner, I was drawn to his eyes. They were a strange color walking a fine line of being green or brown. They invited me into his soul and relaxed me enough to let down my guard.

After brunch, we ended up at one of the many

parks in Atlanta. I couldn't tell you what it was called, but we sat on a blanket by a tree relaxing and conversed about future goals, favorite colors, Bush being in office, and our thoughts on religion and homosexuality. He laid his head in my lap. I stroked his face and played with his dreads. It turned out to be a gorgeous day and evening. The temperature was bearable, and nothing about the date was rushed or forced. We promised to keep in touch, and when ready, plan a visit to see one another.

He took me back to the hotel and walked me to my room. We shared a very passionate kiss. It felt so right. A tingling sensation made its way through every inch of my body. His lips were so soft, and he tasted lovely. He held me firmly as if letting me go would throw him off balance. I had anticipated this moment when I saw him earlier that day. I thanked God for sending this dude into my world. To me, he was the man I had prayed into my life - the epitome of a Black man. Could I be falling already?

A Spade Is a Spade

The trip to ATL was just what I needed. I still had Gary on the brain also. I didn't think I was going to hear anything from him. I did give him a call and left a message on his phone. So the ball was now in his court to call and show some interest...

In the meantime, I continued to kick it with Darius. I couldn't wait to tell him about my trip to Atlanta and how much fun me and the crew had. I had tried to convince him to come with us before we left, but he didn't want to be a part of the gayness as he so eloquently stated. I went over to his crib to tell him about my adventure after work the day after we got back, where he had dinner waiting.

"Darius, Atlanta was off the chain! You should have gone!" I said biting into a hush puppy. "And thank you for the soul food, brotha." Raising my fist in the air.

"You're welcome, I can't believe you been out here this long, and never been to Hilda's," he said referring to the local soul food restaurant in Jacksonville.

"I guess I been sleeping on it. It's cool, but not like my Granny's cooking," I said longing for one of her home cooked meals.

"Ol' white washed face ass."

"Shut the hell up! Ol' ghetto peppermint in the middle of a pickle eating face ass," I said. He laughed stuffing his mouth with greens.

"Yo' so how many niggas you mess with out there?" he asked with a smirk. "I'm staring at a bunch of hickeys on your neck," he asked with a smirk.

"Dude, it ain't even like that. I'm not a ho like you," I said throwing a hush puppy at him.

"So what's up with them love marks on your neck then?" he asked popping the hush puppy in his mouth.

"Boy, ain't no marks on my neck punk!" I said laughing.

"And why I got to be a ho?"

"Darius, I can't go anywhere with you without you flirting or trying to get somebody number. You be trying too hard."

"What you mean trying too hard?" he smiled leaning back on the couch.

"I guess to prove your manhood or something...like you wear it on your sleeve. I mean you're charming, but you over do the whole playa thing. It's not you."

"So what I need to do?" he asked inquisitively.

"Tone that macho crap down. It's not sexy to females, and especially dudes like me who know who they are. That's how I clocked you," I said laughing and then stuffing a piece of chicken into my mouth.

"Whatever dude!"

"You'll learn one day," I said shaking my head.

"Anyway, what was Atlanta like?"

"Just what I said. Fun. The clubs were hot. And any type of dude you could want was there. Kats were all in my ear like headphones," I laughed.

"For real?"

"Yup!" I said nodding my head in an ethnic fashion.

"What were the females like?"

"Dude, you asking the wrong one," I said sucking my teeth.

"Why you sucking your teeth? I know there were some chicks out there."

"Ohhhhh! So you like chicks with dicks, the illusion of femininity. Now the truth comes out!" I said laughing.

"Aww hell naw! Don't even come at me like that, partna."

"Whatever! There were plenty of lesbians there, but none of them broads would be checking out your behind."

"Don't underestimate the kid," he said popping his collar.

"Dee, shut your gay ass up! That's exactly what I'm talking about," I said sipping some sweet tea. "So you're going to convert lesbians now?" I said swallowing and wiping my mouth with a napkin.

"Don't underestimate the power of the dick. Plus, your boy got the gift of gab."

"Wow. You confused straight boys are a trip. And to think I was trying not to peg you as a misogynist."

"Naw, I ain't a misogynist. I just know me. I ain't confused. I'm just curious," he said smirking.

"You don't even believe that. I don't think God does either," I said laughing. I shook my head and looked up

107

towards the ceiling.

"Shut up faggot!" he said laughing.

"I'll be that. That word is a term of endearment coming from you," I said popping my collar.

"You silly. Alright, Jay, tell me something, I need to know."

"What?"

"You ever fucked a girl?"

"Nope!" I stated plainly.

"You ain't ever had no pussy?"

"Nope!" I repeated smiling at him."

"So how you know you ain't into ho's then."

"I just know. It's like, they do nothing for me. I don't get aroused by them. I have no desire to sleep with them. I can't explain it. It's the same as you being attracted to girls and guys. It's just in your psyche."

"Well, what attracts you to niggas?"

"That's a great question. Wow! I never really thought about it." I paused before answering the question. "Hmmm...there is a side of masculinity that women will never understand. I see it clearly. Like, there is a roughness yet gentler side of masculinity that only another man can see. I guess only if you're gay because you're looking at me all strange," I said laughing at the look on his face.

"No, no, no, finish. I was listening to you. I'm trying to follow you. Keep going," he chuckled.

"Okay. It's like this. There is no definitive answer to attraction Darius..."

"Do you feel you were born that way?"

"Yeah, I have always had some type of affixation to guys. I remember being drawn to this dude named Rico in the second grade. It was nothing sexual in nature because you don't know the concept of sex at that age. At least I didn't, but there was something there. I enjoyed being around him and we were as good of friends as second graders can be. I looked at him like he looked at the girls. But as I got older, the feelings towards dudes got stronger and stronger. And of course a sexual desire ensued. So I started to learn more about me and began to figure out what it was and prayed on it. I had to gain my own acceptance. Everyone else can kiss my behind. You get one life and one shot at being who God made you to be. I feel gay folk are here for a divine purpose," I said holding my head up high.

"I got you, but what do you like about men?" He turned over on his stomach and got comfortable as he awaited my response.

"I love the strength and simplicity of a man. I love the swagger of a man. I find comfort and protection in masculinity other than my own. It's deep for me. I can't describe it. That's like asking my Dad, well why he is attracted to women. I'm sure he'd say some half thought out comment like... because that's the way it's supposed to be. You have to look deeper than that. Attraction is attraction just as a spade is a spade. It's in your own make-up!"

"I guess I never really thought about why I'm

attracted to women, but with me it's complicated, Jay."

"How so?"

"Well, I like girls, but I'm more comfortable and at ease with a dude. And being with you is cool because I ain't never really put any thoughts into the whys, but I know I like chillin' with you and shit more than I did my girl. You're easier to talk too," he said reaching over and tapping my knee with his hand.

"Darius, you gotta come into your own understanding and acceptance of who you are and who you want to be with. I'm not here to sway you one way or another. Everyone with a sexuality conflict has to figure it out for him or herself and move on with life. But at least be real with those peeps you choose to be with or sleep with."

"Yeah, you're right," he said, rolling over on his back. He placed one hand behind his head and the other up under his shirt revealing his abs. He propped his legs up on the back of the couch. I glanced down at the trail of hair exposed leading to his dick.

"So are you attracted to both sexes equally, or do you like one more than the other?" I asked averting my eyes away from his crotch.

"Damn, I got to be honest with you!" he laughed. "Dude! I like niggas more than I do the hoes. Now as much as I like pussy, I love ass. I love eating it, licking it, playing with it, fucking it. A nigga's ass is off the chain, but I like masculine niggas. Bottoms like you. That's why I'm in your face all the time," he said.

"Okay," I said rolling my eyes. "You are such a cliché."

"What?!?!? I'm being for real," he laughed. "You just said you like masculine niggas too. Now that I say it I'm a cliché."

"It's how you said it. Like them straight kats, that be like I got all these hoes on my jock nigga, I ain't no punk dawg! It's hilarious." I said with a chuckle.

"I'm just saying I don't want my nigga wearing lip gloss and eyeliner with arched eyebrows and shit," he said smiling.

"That type of dude could be the love of your life, you never know." I said with an exaggerated smile.

"Getting back to attraction, nigga," he said shaking his head, "I ain't into that type of guy."

"Me either, so I feel you," I said laughing.

"You feel me?" he asked grinning.

"I feel you, Dee," I said.

"I'm saying, you showing me a lot and making me challenge and deal with some shit I've been dealing with for a long time. I do know my Pops would be open-minded about the gay thing?"

"Really, how you figure?" I asked curiously.

"That's just how he is Jay. Pops has never been closed minded about anything Lauren and I have done. He always reassures us that we can talk to him about any and everything. He's had to be a mother and a father to us, especially after my mom's died from Cancer. He stepped up to the plate and did what needed to be done. He was like, whatever your venture in life is, be you, and live life to make it count for you. He's off the chain, Jay. You talk about strong," he said looking up at the ceiling. It was as if he had taken that moment to thank God for the sacrifices his dad had made for him and his sister. He had a genuine look of humble gratitude across his face.

"You are so lucky then? Have you talked to him about it?" I could see that he was taking his time to open up and let his guard down with me. I felt honored to share in his feelings and possibly assist him in a breakthrough to gain more comfort in his own skin. Here was a guy that felt he had to carry on a sense of machismo at all times expressing himself emotionally. I felt a need to tread lightly so as not to frighten him back into his shell.

"No, I want to present it to him when I know who I am and what type of relationship I'll be in," he said. His eyes focused on mine.

"I feel you. I wish I had that type of support system. It's like my parents don't even know me because I can't be completely honest with them about this part of my life. I have to hide it from them even though they know I'm gay. In my case my family's good intentions and opinions of my quote unquote lifestyle separates me from them. And they have little to no regard for the hurt they've inflicted on me. Not wanting to know your own child is beyond me," I said shaking my head and rolling my eyes.

"I see. You're a strong black man. I know you'll be fine," he smiled.

"Yup, never let them see you sweat. Yeah, but you still need your family though dude no matter how strong you are. Your family is your foundation. You will be fine also. You just gotta make up your mind, Ol' Greedy Smurf I want a dick and pussy sandwich face ass!"

"Whatever, ol' Celie from the Color Purple, "dear God I'm here" face ass!"

"Why I gotta be Celie?" I laughed.

"Because you are going to overcome. Plus, your poetry is off the chain, so it must be therapeutic for you? Use it as a tool."

"Yeah, it is like my therapy. It's helped me on so many levels."

"You need to do something with it. Publish it or something."

"Yeah, some day," I said. I got up to clear the coffee table. I took the containers to the trash. When I came back to the living room, Darius had Common playing in the background. He was sprawled out on his oversized couch.

"Come lay next to me," he said. He patted the cushion next to him.

"Darius, we're supposed to be studying," I said as I walked over to the couch.

"I know, but come lay next to me for a few minutes." "Dude, what you think this is. I ain't with that gay stuff!" I said jokingly.

"Shiiid! You're like that box of Fruity Pebbles on my fridge! Gayer than a mothafucka!" he said.

"But you're the one eating Fruity Pebbles," I said standing over him.

"That's different," he said pulling me down next to him.

"Yeah, that's a good fag. Staying close to all things rainbow. You're well on your way to becoming a great homosexual."

"Damn, you are not funny at all," he said laughing at me.

"I'm going home punk," I said smiling.

"You ain't going anywhere, homo."

"Well, you'd better laugh at my jokes got-dang it," I said laughing.

"Tell one that's funny then, nigga." He kissed me on my forehead and then on the lips softly. He looked me in the eyes and then proceeded to kiss me deeply. It was the first time we had ever kissed like that before. It was pretty cool. I was not expecting it at all. You could cut the sexual tension between us with a knife but to keep my feelings at bay, I only allowed myself to go so far with him.

"Darius!"

"What?"

"Can you do me a favor?"

"What you need?"

"I need you to admit that you want a dick in your

mouth and a nice pair of heavy balls right about here," I said tapping his chin.

"Get the fuck off me!" he said laughing as he pushed me onto the floor.

"What? You said to tell you something funny!" I said cracking up.

Boarding Passes and Pain

Gary finally called, and he and I talked every day since pride. I would get this huge Kool-Aid grin on my face each time his name appeared on the caller I.D. I had a feeling that this was going to be more than I had initially anticipated. I felt my infatuation turning into something I couldn't quite explain. I didn't want to get ahead of myself until we were in each other's presence away from the magic and allure that Atlanta pride can bring.

There was this amazing drag queen named Misty Blue whom I befriended at a club called Ibiza in Wilmington, North Carolina. She was a gorgeous Mary J. Blige look-a-like that affectionately referred to me as her "Little Chocolate Drop." I loved her because I'm a big Mary fan. She had this warning to share with me: "Beware of the pride bug, baby. Her bite can be filled with one of two things. A nasty dose of poison filled heartbreak, or true love. But it depends on her mood that day. I have seen so many of you young sissies run down to Hotlanta for pride, get all flustered and fall goo-goo eyed in love, rent U-Haul's the following week, only to GAG! So you take your time, honey. Go see what this man is like when recess is over. Let it flow, Chocolate Drop, okay?" I was determined to take her advice and enter into whatever was going on with Gary and me with caution, yet remain optimistic. There is a certain naivety you succumb to when someone is whispering the right shit in your ear.

Not only was Gary whispering the right things in my ear, he was putting his words into action. He surprised me one day during one of our phone conversations by telling me to check my email. He had bought a plane ticket and reserved a room at a really nice hotel in Raleigh. I was floored after opening the attachments and replayed the sexy and aggressive way he seductively ordered, "Get your sexy lil' ass to Raleigh." I immediately put in my leave request and was on pins and needles anxiously awaiting those days to come.

Of course when Michael and Shawn caught wind of our upcoming rendezvous, teasing me became their new pastime. They made it a point to pay me a visit before I left and chanted: "Jason's gonna have some butt sex! Jason's gonna have some butt sex! Jason's gonna have some butt sex! Jason's gonna have some butt sex!"

Gary's flight was on time. I did 90 miles an hour most of the way to Raleigh. I was at the baggage claim waiting with anxiety bubbling within me when I saw him walking toward me. He looked breathtaking as his bright smile broadened when our eyes met. We both had to contain ourselves. So we gave each other the standard black man handshake and hug, but we held on to one another for a little bit. We were still in the Bible belt. He whispered in my ear how he couldn't wait to get me to the room so he could kiss me and hug me for real before releasing me from his embrace. I smiled, almost blushing. I did, however, peck him on the cheek before we let go of one another. Once again the chemistry was off the chain. We jumped back into the groove of one another as if we never left that last night in Atlanta. I felt antsy and super giddy around him. I finally knew what people meant when they speak of butterflies in the stomach. It was a wonderful yet overwhelming feeling. We checked into the hotel, ordered some Chinese food, and immediately dove into one another's mind to dig out a deeper level of conversation.

"I am very comfortable with who I am. Are you comfortable with your sexuality?" I asked. I just knew he was going to give a response similar to the crap Darius was talking about.

"Very much so, I'm a man about mine though. I like my guy to be a little bit soft, but not feminine. There is a difference you know?"

"Yeah, I feel you."

"Like you, I know there is a softer side to you. I can feel it in the way you touch me. You put up this front like you're so tough. Is that from the military?" He smiled and lightly brushed my cheek with his fist.

"Naw, I guess I've always been a loner in a sense. Just trying to understand my sexuality as well as the man I am. I had a senior class of like ninety-eight. And in high school, I always felt like the only one who was gay, you know? I was cool with people but kept to myself for the most part. I was a mystery to the girls. Some of them liked me but couldn't figure out why I wouldn't give them any play, especially when they were blatantly flirtatious. Little whores," I said laughing.

"Leave those girls alone. At least they had good taste in dudes." He smiled and rubbed my leg.

"Perhaps, but I felt that if I would have let people get close to me, they'd discover I was gay, and I would be ostracized. Not to mention, I was hiding it from my parents. That's a whole other story. Man, if it wasn't for prayer, music, and a Mead notebook, I don't know if I would have made it." I surmised. "Your parents know about you, right?" I asked anticipating the story I was about to hear.

"Yes, they both do. I told them after I broke it off with my fiancée. I got tired of fighting with myself and living this big lie to please all of the Caribbean." He laughed. "When I talked to my parents about my decision, they both looked at each other and started clapping."

"What?" I said smiling. "Like a standing ovation or some junk?" I laughed.

"Hell yeah. Clapping! It was the strangest shit. I didn't know what was going on. I think I was twenty-one, no wait, I was 23. I sat them both down. I was scared shitless because you know you can get killed for being gay in the islands. I just knew they'd be against it. I had already told my sisters and my lil' brother. I just came out with it. I said, 'Moms, Pops, I want to explain why I broke it off with Camilla.' I looked at them with

120

tears about to come down my face and I was like, 'It was because I like men."

"Whoa. For real? Like that?" I was in awe. I imagine me being the one telling my parents about my sexuality, but that opportunity was stripped away from me.

"Yup. So these two look at each other. They smile. Then turn to me, they smile again, and start clapping Pops walks over, stands me up, and hugs me. 'Ya think me an yur Mudder don't kno ar' chill'dran. Boy, I knew you was a batty boy lung time ago," he said impersonating his Father's Caribbean accent. "And that was that," he said laughing. "My mom's told me she was waiting for the day I'd be truthful with them. She was all, 'Make sure you find a good one." He chuckled. "Now, they've met my ex Desjardin, the one who I told you broke my heart. And I vowed the next dude I take to meet them would be the actual one. I don't want them to meet mad niggas, you know, at every other family get together and shit. I'm critical about that, you know?"

"Yeah," I smiled. I wondered if he viewed me of being worthy enough to meet his family.

"So, do your parents know about you?" Gary asked.

I took a deep breath. "Yeah, they do now," I sighed. "Dude, they hurt me so bad, that's another reason I keep a wall up.

"Really?" He gave my leg a squeeze.

"Yup! I got a call from my Dad a few months ago. He was telling me that the Lord placed it on his heart to ask me if I was practicing homosexuality," I said rolling my eyes.

"What did you say?" he asked with a worried look on his face.

"I'm not practicing anything. I've got the hang of it now. I'm gay if that's what you want to know," I said. Gary burst into laughter.

"That's some funny shit. You really told your pops that." His eyes searched mine for my response.

"Who? I sure did. I tend to speak my mind, especially when it comes to silly questions like that."

"You didn't have to be so cold about it. He was just trying to handle the situation with some delicacy."

"Maybe, but my momma with her nosy behind, outed me when I was in high school. I played it off as a phase, but I know they knew it wasn't."

"Damn, how'd she do that? What happened?"

My mind went back to the event that caused a rift in my relationship with my parents. It was so vivid. I seemed to zone out as I replayed that day in my head. I had a flashback as I began to tell Gary the story. In an instant, the next few words I spoke seemed as if they'd determined my fate. Suddenly, I felt seventeen all over again...

"I'm only going to ask you this once. Jason. Are you fucking men? You need to tell me the truth because what you say to me right now is crucial. I can't believe what I just found," my mother said as she threw my journal in my lap.

I thought long and hard about what she asked. I wished to God that I were still in my Algebra II class. What the hell was her problem? Why was this a big deal? Her brother is gay, and I don't see her shunning him away! My thoughts jumped back and forth for what seemed like forever. I was starting to break into a cold sweat. I sank in shame deeper and deeper into the leather seat of my mom's car, and it felt as if the world grew colder on that dreary winter day. I felt as if all of Germany knew my horrible secret. She read my journal. I can't believe I was so careless and stupid to leave it sitting on my bed. God, why did I oversleep this morning? How could I have forgotten my journal? I never go any...

"Boy, did you hear what I said?"

"Yes, Ma," I said in a soft shaky voice. I realized that I probably sounded like the faggot she pegged me to be. I repeated my answer with a little more confidence adding more bass in my voice. I think it sounded the same though.

Suddenly the car came to a complete stop. She had pulled over into the parking lot of the Burger King on base. There was complete silence. I noticed that the radio was off. Was this a dream? I turned my head slowly to the left. My eyes made contact with hers. I studied her face in search of sympathy, support, or maybe understanding; only to find a look of disgust, betrayal, and hurt.

"No, Ma, I'm not having sex with men." Thank God I

hadn't, but I was gay. I had never lied to my mother before, but I was going to have to lie this time. Now it was a matter of survival. At this point who knows what she and Dad would have done if I came out to them? I was seventeen years old, in the 11th grade, and what seemed to be a million miles away from the U.S. Her next comment sliced through me like an unsheathed sword.

"I did not raise you to grow up to be a pervert. You are my son, and I'm not going to lose you to AIDS, or God knows what else. Did you notice how different your Uncle looked the last time we were home? I'm handling his affairs now because he's dying of AIDS! And it's because some homo convinced him that this shit was okay. I'm not going to let the same thing happen to my child. I love you! You are my only son! I just don't understand why you want to live a life where you'd have to hide and be so secretive. Is that what you call happiness? Being fucked in the ass, and all types of…." She paused and rubbed her face with her hands. "Lord, PLEASE, tell me why you're doing this to me?"

"Mama, I'm not gay, okay? I was just curious about it, and I'm positive that it is just a phase. I'm sorry. I didn't know about Uncle Jesse either. Mama I'm sorry."

I felt the hurt in her eyes through her empty expression. Without blinking, she took a long deep breath. As her eyes started to water, she asked me, "Have you let…Have you been…having sex with men?" Her eyes never left mine as she waited anxiously for my answer. Her eyes were darting from side to side scanning each one of my eyes.

"No," I responded, praying that at that moment God would expunge my existence.

"Are you confused about your sexuality?" she asked. "No," I stated confidently. I was gay, so no I wasn't confused about that. You just don't want to accept it, lady, I thought to myself.

"Jason, I'm your Mother. If you're confused about something, talk to me! Don't listen to what everyone else is saying, because what they think is good for them, is not always going to be good for you. I raised you better than that, and I'm proud of you, but this is just too much.   I hope you think about what you're doing because what you do affects your family as well as you. Do you understand what I'm saying to you? When we get home we have a lot to talk about. You really need to talk to your daddy when you get home."

It seemed like it took two minutes to drive the 35 miles to our house. There was no traffic on the Autobahn, and I couldn't think of what to say to Daddy. Why did she have to drag him into this? It's bad enough we didn't have the picture perfect father-son relationship. Now, I would have to explain my attraction to men to him. Jesus, please provide me with the strength to face him.

I darted through the door and headed straight to my room. I dropped my bag, and tore off my jacket. Taz, our brown and black Shi-Tzu bounced around my legs, happy to see me, yet eager to go outside. I walked him to the patio door and let him out. I went back to my room and removed my watch and bracelet. I ran to the bathroom. After I relieved myself, I walked over to the sink, turned the water on and washed my hands. I turned the water off and started to dry my hands. I looked in the mirror and noticed the sad look on my face. This was the look I'd had before at my grandfather's funeral. I didn't feel like the same person I saw in the mirror time and time again. I felt like an outcast in my own home, afraid to touch anything. I felt abandoned. What was I supposed to do now? Things will never be the same in this house again. I wished Maria had put me on the schedule to work that day. Then I could focus on work instead of this mess. My mind continued to drift when I heard my father yell out, "Boy, do you hear me calling you."

I walked slowly into the family room. My mom was sitting on the love seat. My dad was sitting on the recliner. I slowly sat down on the couch. The house seemed dark and was totally silent. There was a long pause. I suddenly heard Taz in the background begging to be let in. My mother told me to go and let him in. Not once did my Dad move or even look at me. I opened the door and called out to the dog as he circled the yard. He ran through the door past me to his dish of water in the kitchen. I closed and locked the door. I then took a deep breath and said to myself, whatever happens, be a man, and tell them what they want to hear, you'll be out of this place in a year. Free to be me on my own terms.

I walked back casually with Taz trotting behind me. When I walked through the door, I was welcomed by my father's glare. I couldn't release my eyes from his powerful stare. There was an empty feeling in my stomach as I stared into his eyes. I began to feel uneasy and small. The look was so callous. I'll never forget it. I sat down never once blinking as he spoke the five most hurtful words I've ever heard. "Now I have two daughters." He shook his head and turned away from me. My heart, though beating fast, sank. I dropped my head in preparation for a long night, and quite possibly a long weekend. Aside from feeling persecuted, I remembered thinking: How could I have been so careless that morning?

The Plane, The Plane

"Petty Officer Williams is going to be our new X-ray Technician. So you will take over your new station this morning. I'm going to switch you with Trent. Good to go?" my Supervisor said.

"Yes, Chief!"

"So, Trent, you get with Williams, and he'll show you how to run sick-call and let you know what Commander Dickson expects. Good to go?"

"Got it, Chief," Seaman Trent replied.

"Alright, if no one has anything further to pass, let's turn two. Dental Department! Attention! Dismissed!" My supervisor barked.

Since I had taken the Oral Radiography course, I was now going to be doing my own thing in X-ray. I was happy about being in charge of my own space, and I felt like I could run X-ray better than the last person they had over it. She was a mess. Plus, I needed some leadership credit on my evaluation.

The day started out like any other day. It was a typical muggy sunny morning in North Carolina. I made my way to work. The Department Head brought in Donuts, and I had spoken to Gary on the drive in. We were discussing when I planned on coming out to see him. I was still waiting to see the Command Career Counselor about my orders. I was thinking of popping up there towards the end of the month or early October. I wanted to visit my family in Detroit as well, so I would need to strategically plan this trip.

I had seen four or five patients in addition to taking inventory of my equipment and supplies. At about ten minutes till nine, I noticed people were really glued to the television in the patient waiting area. I walked up to the front desk to shoot the breeze.

"Mrs. Turner, it's slow in here today. What's going on up here? You chasing the patients away?" I said joking with her.

"I was just thinking the same thing. It is a little slow in here, huh? I'm not gonna complain though," she said looking at the clock.

"You know what? I shouldn't either. We could use some down time." I said.

"Exactly! You see this thing on the news, sweetie? About that plane?"

"No, what plane? I've been in X-ray all morning taking inventory," I said.

"Look at the T.V. Some plane crashed into the World Trade Center… smashed right into one of them towers," Mrs. Turner said. She pointed at the T.V. in the main lobby. I walked over to view the news and investigate.

"What? Let me check this out. What was it, a commuter plane or something?"

"They don't know yet. They think it was a commercial airliner," one of the Marines stated.

"Oh really? How in the world could they have done that?" Mrs. Turner questioned. I turned in the direction the patient was seated.

"The pilot may have passed out or something. Oh My God, I wonder if there are any survivors," I said looking back at the screen.

"Man, I don't know, it looks like there is a fire, so an explosion must have happened," the Marine said.

"Yeah, I see all the smoke. Whoa! That's crazy," I said. "Mrs. Turner, I'll be back. I got to finish that inventory this morning," I said placing my hand in my pocket to fish out a stick of gum.

"Alright, if you see Peterson, can you tell him his patient is here sweetie?" she asked.

"Okay, I'll get him," I said right as he was walking up front.

"Man, Williams you see this crap on the news about the jet?" Peterson asked. He pointed to the T.V. shaking his head.

"Yeah, I was just looking at it. How in the world do you accidentally hit the tower?" I asked with a hint of sarcasm.

"I ougn't know kid, but my sistah works down there. I just got off the phone with her. She's in the other tower, so she's fine. But yo' she said she heard it though," Peterson said with his sexy New York accent. He had that rugged look about him like the rapper Red Man.

"Dang you serious?" I asked.

"Yeah, dawg, she said she heard this loud ass boom, and the building shook a little, but yo' she cool. They tryna see what's going on right now though."

"Dang, well man, I'm glad she's alright," I tapped him on the shoulder. "Yeah man, we all each other got dawg! But yo' let me take care of this patient son. I'ma holla." he said.

"Alright man. BROOKLYN!" I shouted pounding my fist on my chest.

"Fo'sho kid!" he said smiling. I walked back to my area and jumped back on the inventory of my supplies. A few minutes later, Chief walked in.

"Petty Officer Williams, come to my office for a minute," she ordered.

"Okay, Chief."

"You don't have any patients do you?" she said poking her head in through the door.

"No, not at the moment," I answered. I sat my clipboard on the desk and proceeded behind her as she opened the door for me.

"Alright, I just want to go over some information with you. Have a seat," she said as we walked into her office.

"Now you still want to get into the hygiene program, right?" She put her eyeglasses on her face.

"Of course I do." I smiled.

"How far along are you with the classes they require?"

You've already started one class right?"

"I am taking the chemistry right now. I have a month left. I finished the microbiology and the human

132

anatomy and physiology a few weeks ago," I said with confidence. I was also able to occupy some of my time in Japan to knock some general studies out, so I was ahead of the game in some respects.

"Good to go. So you're not playing around, huh?" she smiled.

"Not at all, Chief," I chuckled.

"Okay, I need you to pass that class so that we can get you into this program. What I am going to do is push for your orders to Great Lakes and start putting your package together, okay? I'll talk to Kowalski," she said. She grabbed a pen and jotted something down on her desk calendar.

"Okay, Chief, that sounds like a plan," I said smiling.

"Okay. I'm pulling some strings to get you into the program ahead of a bunch of people because I know you want this and you've really done an outstanding job since you've been here. I need you to continue doing that, and bust your ass in this class.... excuse my French. Okay?"

"Got it, Chief." I smiled.

"You do your part, and I'll do mine. Now I will have a write up for you to do, and I'm gonna print that out for you now. I need you to complete as much info as you can. I need dates, awards, volunteer work on and off duty, collateral duties, classes, and grades, what you've done in the Navy, all that okay?"

"Yes. So have that to me by Thursday, and don't worry about your orders. That's the easy part. I got you, okay? I know some folks."

"You got me, Chief?"

"Hey, you know if I say it, it's done alright? Now you just do what you have to do, and I'm gonna help make this happen, okay?"

"Yes, Chief."

"Okay, I also need a bio from you as well. That's part of the write up. Other than that, do you have any questions?"

"Not at the moment, Chief?"

"Okay, let me print this out for you?" She smiled and took her eyeglasses off.

"Chief, what's going on with this plane thing? Did you see that?"

"Yeah, they were saying something about it on the radio too. They said it might have been a missile or something like that. I don't know?"

"Okay let me get this, I think it's jammed...no there it goes. I need to have Perez order me a new printer. I don't know about this thing." She said shaking her head.

"It's always something, ain't it?" I laughed.

"I'm telling you. Man, this thing has really been acting like it wants to call it quits." She laughed.

"Chief, I was wondering if..."

"OH FUCK NO! MY SISTER IS IN THERE, MAN, HELL NO!" Chief and I recognized the voice. It was Peterson. Her office was within close proximity to the front desk. She rushed out of the office to investigate the outburst.

"Hey, hey, hey, what's going on? Is all that cursing necessary in front of patients?" Chief scolded.

"I'm sorry, Chief, but my sister is in there, she works in that building!" Peterson said. He was visibly upset and shaken as he pointed at the screen. His eyes were red and welling up with tears.

"What happened?" Chief asked abruptly.

The other tower got hit by a plane too. It's on the news!" Mrs. Turner explained. I heard them talking and rushed out to the waiting area to look at the T.V. Most of the staff had gathered there.

"Oh my God!" I said. The footage replayed the second plane hitting the other tower. Peterson was standing there with his hands on his head, teeth clenched, face flushed, breathing heavily.

"Peterson, go into my office and call your sister. See if you can get a hold of her. Okay? Come on. Let's not think the worst just yet okay?" Chief said as she guided him to her office and closed the door.

She came back to join the crew a few moments later. We were all in shock. CNN had our full-undivided attention with a caption that read: "Terrorist Attack on the World Trade Center." No one moved. We were all anxious to know who did this, and why? This was truly something you'd see in a movie depicting the end of the world.

I couldn't believe my eyes. There they were. The North and South towers. The World Trade Center standing tall with two gaping holes pouring smoke into

135

the sky. America seemed to come to a halt. We had no choice but to take notice and watch in shear horror listening to the media with prescient thoughts. Within minutes, it was confirmed that this was indeed a terrorist attack. Peterson walked into the waiting room and stood next to Leyah and I. He looked as if he was going to lose it.

"I can't get through. The lines are busy. And the cell phones are down or something. It keeps saying all circuits are busy. Damn, this shit can't be happening, dawg! My sister is in there, bruh!" Peterson said gesturing towards the television.

"Dude, let's just stay calm for the time being. I know it's a lot running through your mind, but let's channel some positive energy her way," I said, as he nodded his head never once taking his eyes off of the screen.

"Keep trying Peterson, okay?" Leyah said.

I walked back to X-ray to grab my phone out of my bag. I attempted to make a call home, but I got the same message that Peterson had mentioned. All circuits are busy. I placed the phone in my pocket and walked back out front.

Our Department head was watching alongside the staff. We were all commenting on the events. All very anxious and very confused. One couldn't help but feel helpless while different events just kept occurring one after the other. There was an explosion at the Pentagon and the White House was evacuated. We saw footage of individuals jumping to their demise in an attempt to free themselves from the fires within the building. There was also footage of evacuees. Peterson was hoping to get a glimpse of his sister. He had received a call from one of his aunts. She informed him that she had been trying to call him and still could not get a hold of his sister Alicia. He was trying his best to keep his composure. Then the South Tower began to collapse and disintegrate into nothing.

Chief pulled him back into her office to calm him again. A couple of the staff members including Leyah started crying. I went to get some Kleenex for them. Leyah asked me why this was happening. I didn't have an answer. She placed her arm around me and laid her head on my shoulder. I put my arm around her as well trying to offer her comfort. We continued watching the news. Approximately thirty minutes later, the second tower collapsed.

Our department head received a call that the base was on lock down until further notice. He instructed us to secure the clinic and get ready to head home. They would be releasing everyone as soon as the okay was given. We would be doing a phone muster that night and the next morning to inform everyone if they needed to come in or not.

The building was silent as we quickly shut things down, changed clothes, and ran back up front to see what else was happening. The news media recounted the morning's events over and over. I tried calling Gary and everyone else I could think to call but was unsuccessful. I could see that I had voicemails but could not access those either. What did America do to deserve this? Tuesday, September 11, 2001, a day we will never forget. It made me really take a look at myself, my surroundings, and what mattered most to me in life. Gary was the first person I thought about. I wanted to cling to him at that moment and know that everything was going to be alright. My second thought was that if we were going to go to war, I would be down for the cause. After all, I was a member of the armed forces.

When we finally got the word from headquarters, my department head sent everyone home to be with their loved ones. Everyone was still numb and in a state of disillusion. I was still trying to dial out only to receive a busy signal or a voice telling me that all circuits were busy. I began thinking that maybe they attacked the phone lines or satellites. This was crazy.

Peterson still had not heard from his sister. He was able to speak with his aunt again. They still had not heard from her. They also could not get down to the lower Manhattan area to see if she was one of the survivors evacuated from the buildings before they collapsed. He was still keeping the faith, but dude was all torn up inside.

I finally made my way off of the base. I didn't want to go back to the barracks because I didn't want to be alone. I decided to go to Michael's place and be around those I cared about. I jumped when I heard the phone ring. It was Gary calling. I quickly answered the phone relieved that he was there with me in spirit.

After the Dust Settles

The next few weeks were a whirlwind of emotion and the media's take on the President's series of regrouping strategies. Though there was a measure of confusion post 9-11, one thing was certain. The war on terrorism was about to commence. While we all tried to return to our normal everyday lives, there was something different in the air. There was a heaviness that was hard to lift.

There was a loss that hit home. My shipmate, Peterson, did in fact lose his sister on that fatal day. She was twenty-five years old. She had just completed her master's degree. She was engaged to be married and was ready to start her career in accounting and finance. She was on one of the floors hit by the airliner. As expected, Peterson took the news very hard. He had lost his parents a few years back to a house fire. Now his big sister was taken from him. Our hearts went out to him and his family. The staff offered him great support. We sent a beautiful floral arrangement and took up a monetary collection for him to cover his travel expenses. He took some time off to be with his family. It was definitely a reality check for us. This was indeed a real event that had taken place and affected real people.

I had to take care of some paperwork at my unit's headquarters building before my trip to Detroit and Chicago. I had to catch a flight out of Raleigh, so Shawn and Michael drove me to the airport. On the way Shawn asked if I had heard from Lyzell. We had a falling out of sorts before the Atlanta trip over some things that I said about him being too much of a queen for me to handle on a daily basis. I felt bad for saying it after the fact because deep down it really hurt his feelings, but I could only handle Lyzell in doses. Small doses in fact. Shawn knew I wasn't going to budge on the issue at hand because of my own stubbornness. With that being said, he made it a point to keep me in the know on the latest foolery surrounding Lyzell in hopes that I'd cave in and rekindle the friendship. He felt that if he kept talking about him from time to time, I wouldn't miss out on knowing who he was. I suspect he kept Lyzell abreast with the latest news in my world as well. So it was no surprise when Shawn told us the story of his discharge from the Marine Corps on the way to the airport.

"Okay! So chile you know Lyzell left the other day, right?"

"He was going back to Virginia, right? I asked. I placed the cap back onto a bottle of water I was sipping on.

"Um hmm. He left late yesterday morning. It was a kee kee." Shawn shook his head and laughed to himself.

"Why? What happened?" I said focusing my attention on Shawn.

"He actually left around my lunch time. I got a call from that whore telling me to come outside to meet him in the parking lot. Chile, I get down there, and this big queen is modeling next to the biggest moving truck they make. Bitch, he spilled all my tea," Shawn said adjusting his necklace.

"You know that big Nellie is good for that," I laughed. "That's why I can't deal with that ho." I continued laughing imagining Lyzell acting a fool.

"I know right!" Shawn said.

"What did he do?" I asked shaking my head.

"So you know it was lunch time, right?"

"Uh huh," I said anticipating what was to come.

"So this queen is wearing a pair of the tightest jeans he could find in his closet. He had one of those do-rags with the long back, swinging like it was a ponytail, and kept saying, "Girl, this," and "Girl, that," and you know how loud that whore is."

"I know right! The human mega phone," I replied.

"So this queen jumps in the truck and goes, 'Okay girl, I'll call the girls later and make sure you ain't going to Pakistan, girl. Bye, cunt!' he blows the horn, and drove off. Chile, all I hear is BOMP! BOMP! 'Say hi to the girls over in Paki for me'! Jason I gagged and then kee kee'd," he said bursting into laughter and shaking his head.

"That big country woman! Oh my God. Lyzell is a trip!" I said. Michael and I joined in on the laughter.

"Jason, I was so embarrassed. Leave it to Lyzell to go out with a bang. In the biggest U-Haul truck, she could find." he said laughing. "BOMP! BOMP! Say hi to the girls over in Paki!" Shawn said laughing and shaking his head.

"Wow!" I said. "Is that going to be the new phrase?" I laughed.

"Okay chile! I kee kee'd. So what's the tea with you and Gary?"

"Oh, we're good. He is worried that I'm going to go to war or some tea. I'm like, boy, don't trip on that. I am on my way to a non-operational unit soon, so your boy is safe for now, but I did tell him if I have to go then, that's the way it is. I am in the Navy. It's hard trying to explain that to folk who aren't in, you know?"

"I know right? You got your orders yet?"

"Of course. Chile Operation Chicago is still in full effect. We were about twenty minutes away from the airport. I am going to spend a few days with my family. Then rent a car and drive to Chicago to spend the latter part of my time with Gary."

Things with Gary were going great and moving at a nice pace for the most part. I was once again preparing for a new start. That was the beauty of the military. You could always pack up and try a new place every couple of years.

It had been some time since I had visited the family. I was looking forward to visiting some of my relatives. The current times really made you take a closer look at what should be important and who should matter to you. So even though I felt estranged from my family in certain aspects, it was always a good idea to right wrongs and keep trying to develop a since of closeness at least in my opinion. At any rate, it was going to be great being on vacation and taking a break from the monotony of the daily grind. Of course Michael, being the big brother to us all, joked with me about not going AWOL (Absent Without Leave) once I got to Chicago and around Gary.

"So what I want to know is: Are you going to give up that ass?" Michael asked. He looked over at me awaiting my response before focusing his attention back on the road. I looked at him, with my mouth agape.

"Wow! You just put it out there like that?" I said smiling. I wondered why I was so surprised.

"You know how we do, ho! Don't act brand new," Michael stated.

"I mean, I don't know. I guess if it happens it happens. I want to do it, but I don't know," I said. At that point, I was blushing unclear of a definite answer.

"Have ya'll talked about it?" Shawn asked inquisitively. He had a curious smirk on his face as he moved to the center seat. He rested his arms on the seat backs.

"We've talked about it in a roundabout sort of way. Surprisingly the sex topic hasn't been a motivating factor in our conversations," I said looking at him.

"Well, that might be a good thing. So he probably does want more with you," Shawn stated.

"Umm hmph! He gon' try to slip it in as soon as you

get to Chicago. Just be prepared. You do your part and make sure that booty hole is squeaky clean," Michael said abruptly.

"Michael, shut up! Not everybody is a gut bucket skeezer like you," I said. I gave his shoulder a punch as I sucked my teeth.

"I'm just telling you from a top's perspective. He's gonna have you in his territory too! Oh yeah, he gon' rape your lil' ass if you come all that way and deny the booty. So um… just bite the pillow and toot it up!" Michael said laughing.

"What a mess you are. I'll keep that in mind," I said rolling my eyes and smiling. Michael was notorious for being blunt when it came to sex. A free spirit in the bedroom might be too mild a term to describe his sexual prowess.

"Well, whatever you do, wrap it the hell up!" Michael said. His tone turned from jovial to serious.

"Oh you know I will. I mean, if the chemistry is right, I think it'll be cool. You know? To go there with him," I smiled and shrugged my shoulders.

"Awww, Jay is gonna finally get that booty beat up. Oooh, he gon' dig you out! You know that right? There ain't nothing like some good ol' virgin booty!" Michael said. He squealed in sheer delight as his body shook.

"Okay, let's change the subject, cause you know this whore is good for going on and on about sex," Shawn said shaking his head laughing.

"Chile, booty is a wonderful thing, especially if it's

good," Michael said. He reached over to pinch my cheek.

"Chile, a mess honey," Shawn said. He leaned back in the seat.

We finally made it to the airport. I hugged the two of them, grabbed my bags, and made my way through security. I ended up putting my ear buds in and slept the entire flight. The flight attendant politely tapped me on the shoulder to wake me up before we made our final descent. I was excited yet nervous at the same time. My dad's side of the family was all going to be together. I had not seen them or my parents for quite some time. The majority of both sides of the family still lived in Detroit, so it was pretty nice to come to one city and see everyone in one trip.

I was wondering how thick the tension was going to be between my Dad and I. I mean, he and my mother now knew that I wasn't playing about this same gender-loving thing. Now it was just one other thing we didn't talk about. The last conversation he and I had was very awkward due to him going off on a tangent about how wrong it was. He also thought it necessary to tell me how this "lifestyle" was a choice. I almost hung up on him. We as black gay men are not allowed to pursue or act out these feelings and urges we have like our heterosexual counterparts. A lot of the shame and guilt stems from the fact that we are forced to hide our true selves, which equates to an initial skewed identity.

It trips me out how straight folk classify being gay as

a lifestyle. My dad makes it seem as if screwing multiple women and having two or three illegitimate children would be more Christ like. Every time he calls, he always asks the same stupid question. "So how them girls out there treating you?" I always respond with the same smart answer. "The same way they treat their hairdresser, I suppose." This always ends the macho heterosexual portion of the conversation. One day, he'll take the hint. Michael burst out laughing one day when he heard me tell him that, but I don't have time to play pretend anymore. Respect me and who I am and I'll return the favor. I made sure I rented a car for this very reason. I told Gary to be on stand-by because if he pissed me off, I'd be making an early trip to Chicago. He encouraged me to tough it out.

I picked up my luggage, the rental car, and hit the road. The first stop was going to be my grandmother's house. I received a call from a number I didn't recognize. I didn't owe anyone any money, so I answered it as I made my way onto the freeway.

"Hello," I said cautiously.

"Thank God, my baby made it safely. I was holding my breath the whole time," Gary said.

"Oh yeah, so you spent three hours with no air and you're still alive?" I asked. I was smiling ear to ear. Hearing Gary's baritone made me relax and set my mind at ease. I could not wait to see this man again.

"See how good God is?" he chuckled. I could picture his smile in my head.

"High Glory! Praise him!" I said laughing. I looked down at my speed and slowed the car down.

"You a fool boy! You alright?"

"Yeah, I slept the whole way here," I said.

"So you wasn't scared or nothing?" He asked with concern in his voice.

"It's not that serious. We can't be afraid to live in our own country. Security was mad crazy though. I had to do everything but give a urine sample."

"Oh yeah? What did they make you do?"

"Oh my God, baby. You gotta take off your shoes, your belt, and empty everything in your pockets. They barely want you to bring a carry-on bag, so they measure it. If it's bigger than this little box thing they have set up, you have to check it. Then they make you do the hokey pokey while bending over so your knees touch your elbows. It was terrible." I said embellishing the latter part of my experience.

"So they are tripping, huh?" Gary chuckled.

"For the most part," I said looking over my shoulder so that I could switch lanes.

"So you ready to see your family?"

"No, but I'm ready to see you?" I said taking a deep breath.

"Not that that's a bad thing, but why me and not the fam?"

"I just don't want to end up going off on somebody, especially my dad. And ever since I can remember, my grandma gives me this judgmental look. I don't know." I took a slight pause thinking. "Maybe that's all in my head, but I know my dad has talked to her about me. And I told you if my dad goes for it, I'm going to go for it. I know it's my grandma's birthday and all, but Gary! I swear!" I said finally taking another moment to breathe.

"Jason! Baby! Your energy is real negative right now. Now if you go visiting your folk with that mindset, the slightest thing is going to set you off babe. You feel me?"

"Yeah...you're right," I sighed again checking my speed.

"You ain't feelin' me," he said laughing. I could picture him cocking his head to the side. He had done this a couple of times before when he was trying to get through to me.

"What you mean?" I asked innocently. "I hear what you're saying. I'll change my tune and expect the best not the worst, but I'm telling you..."

"Nope, we're going to get you through this Jay. Ain't gon' be no buts," Gary stated with firm authority.

"I like your nerve!" I had to admit it turned me on. It was a good thing he couldn't see my response. I'm sure he would have seized the moment.

"Uh huh, and I like you, lil' feisty ass," he said.

"I like you too."

"How you gon' show me?" he asked seductively.

"By coming to see you."

"Oh yeah, you coming now right?"

"I can't yet boo. I have to do the family thing first," I

responded in a cutesy type of tone.

"Damn! I'm looking forward to holding you and being all up on you. You know that?" he said.

"Yeah, me too. I'm scared though." I was more so nervous than anything. The possibility of taking the relationship to the level of having sex was a big deal. I didn't know how to address that with him just yet until I figured out the bottom line.

"What are you scared of?" I could hear him adjust the phone.

"I don't know. It's like.... I'm going to be in your territory," I said.

"I know right? Damn, you got my dick hard," he said laughing.

"See what I'm saying. That's what I'm talking about," I said. I was a little embarrassed by my response.

"You'll be safe. I got you. Don't be skeer'd," he chuckled.

"Umm hmm. And what number is this you're calling me from?" I asked, attempting to change the subject.

"This is my work number, so save it in your phone," he said.

"What! I get the work number? That's hot! I guess I'm doing something right, huh?" My smile was so broad, I'm sure he could tell through the phone.

"Yeah, maybe. We'll see how you act when you get the CHI-town experience," He stated in a coy manner.

"I know right. Things may change," I laughed.

"Well listen, baby, I got to get back to work, so I'll get at you later, a'ight?"

"Okay, you have a good day."

"I will. Jason, keep your cool with the family. A'ight?"

"I'll try. I can't promise you anything."

"See you looking to pick a fight," he said laughing. "Not really," I said.

"Put it like this, whether your family loves it or hates it, at the end of the day you're still gay. You don't have a choice in dealing with it. They do. You can't force things on people," Gary said.

"Yeah, but I can demand my respect as a man though."

"And you have every right to do that. I totally agree babes, but don't get all worked up about closed minds towards reality. There is a period of adjustment for shit like this Jay."

"Gary, that's easy for you to say. Your family has your back. I'll talk to you later."

"A'ight, shorty," he said hanging up the phone.

I drove into the city limits of Detroit. It was strange how things looked so different each time I visited. It looked to be a little cleaner this time around. It looked as if the new mayor was trying to rejuvenate the city. Maybe in five or six more years, my hometown would be back on the map. The mayor was taking over where Mayor Coleman Young left off. He intended to bring more revenue into the city through the building of the

MGM Grand Casino. There was a renovation project happening downtown as well as a re-pavement project of the city's streets and freeways. Now if the big three would build a car Americans would be proud to drive, which lasts longer than three and a half years, they would really be in business.

I made a pit stop at a corner store down the street from Grandma's. I just had to get a bag of barbeque flavored Better Maid Potato chips, a pack of Hostess Orange Cupcakes, and an ice cold Faygo Redpop. I planned on getting a sandwich later from this restaurant called The Bread Basket. They sold the best open-faced corned beef sandwiches I've ever tasted. And the sandwiches are the size of your head. Hopefully, I wouldn't completely blow my diet and undue my exercise routine while on vacation, but my inner fat boy seemed to have other plans.

I found a spot in front of my grandma's house and parked the car. I shut the engine off and took a deep breath. I kept telling myself to think positive thoughts. It was going to be alright. I removed the keys from the ignition and grabbed my bag of goodies. I put a smile on my face, traveled up the walkway, up the porch steps, and rung the doorbell. A few moments later I heard my aunt Rayna yell out, "Lil' Jay here, ya'll!" She unlocked the door to let me in.

"Come here boy, let me hug your neck!" she said laughing. This was her way of teasing me. When I was little, I would always say she was hugging me neck.

"Hey, Auntie, how are you?" I said. It was really good to see her. I had a huge Kool-Aid grin on my face as we embraced. She was a short, stout woman with a smooth virtually flawless almond complexion. She was now rocking a short styled haircut with a swoop bang flowing to the right side of her beautiful round face. Her laugh and charismatic nature could bring out the best in anyone. She had a wonderful spirit and was the baby sister.

"I'm good baby! Look at you! I got a handsome lil' nephew. Ol' short self," she said taking a step back to look at me. She grabbed on to my hand.

"I'm still taller than you. Nah!" I said laughing.

"Alright, don't get popped. You're barely taller than me," she emphasized, "and I see you went and bought a bag full of junk. If you're hungry, you might want to wait. We'll be eating when everybody gets back."

"Yeah, I haven't eaten since last night. I'm scared to eat before I fly," I said rubbing my stomach.

"Why?" she laughed.

"Cause I refuse to use those bathrooms on the plane. They are all cramped and nasty. I can't do it," I said as we both laughed.

"I don't blame you, baby," Aunt Rayna said. She shook her head and pursed her lips as she turned and walked away from the entrance of the house. I followed in behind her.

"Hey, L. J., what's up? I'm glad you made it," my cousin Shayna said as she hugged me followed by my other cousin Maya. Shayna was Aunt Rayna's daughter, and Maya was my Aunt Tina's daughter, my dad's oldest sister.

"What's going on, chicks?" I said enthusiastically. I kissed and hugged them both tightly. "I've missed you gals."

"We missed you too. You need to visit more often," Shayna said rolling her neck and giving me Detroit girl attitude. She was starting to develop into a shapely young woman. You could see the battle the sassy womanhood within her was waging with her girlish innocence. She had the same smooth almond colored complexion, as Aunt Rayna, beautiful dough eyes and a smile and laugh just like her Mother. Aunt Rayna refused to let her wear her hair down in fear that she might look to grown. She was definitely going to be a heartbreaker.

"I know I do. When I move to Chicago, I'll be down more often." I said. I put my hand on my hip and rolled my neck mocking Shayna. She sucked her teeth and smiled.

"Oooh you're moving? Can I come and stay with you?" Maya asked. Maya was just as pretty, but she was a slimmer version of Shayna, and wore glasses. She was a year younger than Shayna, and wanted to do almost everything she did. The girls had a close bond with one another, which to me was a great thing. They were two peas in a pod. The only difference is, Maya was allowed to wear her hair down from time to time. Aunt Tina, who was at work, liked to have girls' night out with the two of them every other weekend.

"What you gon' do about school little girl. You're only 14?"

"I can go to a Chicago school. And in the summertime, I can come back here to visit Mama and everybody. We can work this right on out," she said trying to sound grown up.

"We'll see. I don't know if I can deal with your spoiled tail though. You're a handful," I said putting her in a headlock. We both sat down on the couch. My aunt went into the kitchen. A few moments later, I heard water running and a few pots rattling.

"I'm not as spoiled as you are. And anyway I know what I want and I get it, that don't make me spoiled." She smiled.

"Well, I hear differently," I said. I jabbed her forehead with my index finger.

"How long will you be here, cousin?" Shayna asked. "Just a few days... I have to go to Chicago to check out the base and get a feel for the school I'm going to."

"What school?" Shayna asked.

"College of Lake County. I'm going to be doing my clinicals for the Dental Hygiene program."

"Ugh! You want to be cleaning people mouths all day," Shayna said. She had a grimace on her face.

"Yeah, it's pretty good money in that."

"Ugh. I couldn't be smelling nobody bad breath all day. Is that what you do in the Navy?" Shayna asked.

"Not exactly. I know how to do it. But I work in the X-ray Department at my clinic." I said. I shook my head and laughed at her because the look on her face was too funny.

"You like it?" Shayna asked.

"Yeah, I love dental stuff. It's pretty chill. Plus, it's paying the bills."

"What ya'll want to be?" I asked.

"I want to be a nurse like Aunt Janet."

"Ugh! You want to be changing bed pans all day?" I said laughing.

"Shut up boy! That's not what they do. That's what the CNA's do." Shayna said. "I'm going to be the head nurse." She stated matter of factly.

"Ohhhh, so somebody did a little research? So you do listen to me," I said laughing.

"Always. Don't play!" she laughed hitting me upside the head.

"Alright, alright!" I said.

"Me and my girl Kaneitra are gonna go to the same program in Highland Park."

"Oh yeah?"

"Yup! I got it all mapped out."

"Your daddy and them will be back shortly, LJ They had to take Mama to get her dress and run a couple of last minute errands," Aunt Rayna said. She came and sat with me and my cousins in the living room. "Your Uncle Darnell, Robbie, and, Cee Cee will be here after while from Saginaw too."

"So everybody will be here! Good!" I said.

"Where's my new Uncle?" I asked inquiring about her husband.

"Marcus is at work. You actually just missed him, baby. He'll be back late tonight, so you might not see him until tomorrow."

"Does he still work for Ford?" I asked.

"Uh huh. It will be five years now. When was the last time you saw Robbie, LJ?" she asked rubbing my head. Robbie was my cousin. We were about a year and a half apart in age. When we were kids and they'd come down from Saginaw, we were inseparable.

"It's been a good lil' minute.... like maybe right before we left for Germany," I said.

"You know what, you're right, at the family reunion that year, huh? Well, I'm glad you made it. He gon' be happy to see you."

"Yeah I can't wait to see him either. Where is Jasmine?" I asked, wondering about my sister's whereabouts.

"She up stairs knocked out with her chubby self," my aunt said laughing.

"Are you serious? Naw, she gon' have to wake it on up!" I said standing to my feet.

"She in the guestroom. Come on let's go get her," Shayna said grabbing my hand. We walked up the stairs to the room she was occupying. Maya followed behind us. Jasmine was snoring with a bit of drool leaking from her parted lips. My cousins and I laughed silently to ourselves. I grabbed my phone from my pocket, and searched for my call tones. I selected one and held the phone up to her ear. I pushed the button to make it sound off. Her eyes bugged out, and her body tensed as the three of us all burst into laughter.

"Ya'll play too much. Dang!" Jasmine said in a groggy voice. She sat up, rubbed her eyes, and started stretching as she got her bearings.

"Wake yo' lazy behind up, heffa! You gon' sleep your life away. You're on vacation. Get it on up!" I said shaking her. I noticed that she had put on some weight. She was a pretty brown skinned girl who looked more grown than I'd remembered. She was turning into a young woman with the thick figure and full breast to match. I didn't know how to adjust to the fact that my little sister was not so little up top anymore. She had the same beauty mark on her face as Mama, and she had a slight bow legged pigeon toed stance.

"Be quiet. I was tired. When did you get here?" she said reaching out to hug me.

"Not too long ago. And don't be touching me with that drool on your face and hands, Ugh! Go on somewhere!" I said as she latched on to me kissing my cheek and laughing.

"Whatever. You know you love me!" she said as we all walked out of the room. She went to the bathroom just as my phone rang. I answered it.

"Hello."

"You playing nice?" Gary asked. He let out a slight

laugh.

"So far so good. I'm mad you checking up on me," I smiled. Again I got butterflies in my stomach from the tone of his voice. It felt great to be thought about from someone you were intimate with.

"That's my job as your man, right?" he asked.

"Is that what you are?" I joked.

"I'ma fuck you up!"

"Try it!"

"You wait till you get here. I see I gotta show you who runnin' thangs!"

"Riiiight! I'll let you think that," I said taking a seat on the bed.

"You just wait. I didn't want anything. I just needed to hear your voice again. And more importantly, see if you were still mad at me," Gary wondered.

"I wasn't mad. I was just making a point," I said. I was touched that he called concerned that I was upset with him. I knew he meant well. The issues I have with my folks are pretty touchy for me. My animosity towards them is definitely something that I need to address somehow.

"So that's why you just ended the conversation all abruptly?"

"I'm not mad. It's just frustrating," I defended.

"I know it is," he sighed.

"Alright, I'll be good. I promise."

"Alright. Call me later," he said kissing the phone.

"I will. Bye!"

"Alright, Jay!" he said as he hung up.

Jasmine came downstairs refreshed and smiling. She sat next to me, put her arm around me, and laid her head on my shoulder. I put my arm around her and leaned my head onto hers. We both took a deep breath and let out a loud sigh. We both broke out into laugher.

"You so silly. girl!" I said still laughing. "You did it too!" Jasmine said.

"I know right. So what's new with you?" I said.

"Nothing, just ready to graduate. We took our senior pictures last week. I have to send you some when they come back. I think they're going to be real cute," Jasmine said.

"Oh yeah, when do they come back?" I asked. I turned towards her and grabbed the locket that was around her neck.

"They told us in about three weeks."

"Oh yeah? How are your mama and daddy doing?"

"They're your parents too, big head. They're doing alright."

"You and Mama still butting heads."

"No, but Daddy still don't like my boyfriend," she said rolling her eyes. I shook my head and laughed.

"He ain't supposed to like your boyfriend. That's how fathers are designed. It's in their nature to protect their daughter from unsightly predators," I said laughing. I pinched her cheek.

"Anyways! He could at least be a little nicer to him. He hasn't even tried to get to know him," Jasmine said.

She rolled her eyes and sighed.

"For real? Why doesn't he like him?"

"I don't know. It all started when he was late picking me up for the homecoming dance."

"Oh yeah, Mama told me about that," I laughed.

"Shut up! It's not funny LJ. Daddy really embarrassed me," she said with disdain.

"What does he look like? You got a picture of this negro," I asked, trying to lighten the mood. Her mood instantly changed and her face brightened. She must have really liked this guy.

"Yeah, hold on. I have to go and get my purse." Jasmine said. She got up and ran upstairs. Maya turned the T.V. to BET's 106 & Park.

"Auntie, I'm hungry!" I yelled out. Aunt Rayna was in the dining room. She was talking on the phone and setting the dinner table.

"As soon as they get here, we can eat baby. Shoot, I'm hungry too. Don't you eat that junk food though," she instructed.

"I'll try not to," I said sticking my tongue out at my cousin Maya. She was looking at me shaking her head and smiling. Jasmine returned and sat down next to me. She was digging in her purse in search of her wallet. Once she found it, she opened it and pulled out a glossy 3x5 portrait.

"This is him?" Jasmine said smiling. She handed me the photo depicting the two of them together. They were in a loving embrace with their faces looking towards the camera. The photo had them framed within the confines of a heart. He was wearing a blue oversized Polo sweater. He had two gold fronts on his lateral incisors. He had a thin goatee outlining a set of thick lips, he was light skinned, wore a short tapered cut, and had chinky dark brown eyes. Judging from the picture, I determined he was definitely straight.

"This Grand's biscuit head boy is the one that got you all sprung?" I joked. To me, he wasn't as cute as my sister made him out to be, but as they say beauty is in the eye of the beholder. He was a'ight, but not my type. He definitely was no competition for my baby.

"Shut up! Don't be talking about my man like that."

"Jasmine, the boy has gold fronts. He looks hood. I see why daddy can't take him serious," I said. Shayna and Maya started laughing.

"Whatever! Give me my picture back," she said snatching the picture from my fingertips. She carefully placed it back within the safety of her wallet.

"Well, if you like him, I love him. I guess I can't say anything negative until I meet him. How long ya'll been together?" I smiled.

"Exactly! We haven't been together that long... officially a little over seven months," she said admiring herself in her pocket mirror.

"What's ol' biscuit heads name, and how old is he?" I asked as she hit my arm. She sucked her teeth as I chuckled.

"You got one more time, Jason!" she said smiling

and shaking her fist at me to affirm her threat was not to be taken lightly. "His name is Khalil, and he's twenty," she replied.

"Twenty, Jas? I am mad at that. You couldn't find a nice high school boy? Captain of the basketball team, perhaps?"

"No! They're all so young acting. I don't have time for games," she said trying to convince me that Khalil was a more appropriate choice.

"Oh so you just grown now, huh? Can't tell you nothing, huh?" I said laughing.

"Nope! You surely cannot!" She said brushing her shoulders off.

"Whatever! And what you call yourself doing to your hair?" I said touching it.

"I had to cut it. I fell asleep with some gum in my mouth and it got stuck in my hair, so I had to cut it. It's cute isn't it?" Jasmine said. She turned her head from side to side so that I could get a good look at it. I was used to seeing her with long flowing hair, so this was definitely different.

"It's cool. I gotta get used to it, I guess. I am mad that you had a wad of gum in your hair." I said shaking my head.

"It was all along the back of my hair. It had spread. I cried like a baby when they cut it." Jasmine said.

"Wow! You poor thing. I know you were traumatized when you woke up and saw that, huh?" I said stroking her hair.

"Come up stairs for a minute." She said grabbing my hand. We both got up from the couch. She led me back upstairs to the guest room. She sat me down and lowered her head. I looked at her searching for a quick clue that would reveal her angst. We talked about all kinds of things, so she knew she could come and talk to her big brother about whatever. I rubbed her back as she turned to look at me.

"Girl, what's wrong with you?"

"I got something to ask you, but I don't know how too."

"Jasmine, just spit it out. We've never been scared to talk to each other, so go for it."

"Well, this isn't easy for me. First off, I need you to know that I love you no matter what. I hope you have the same kind of love for me?" she said. Her breathing became heavy and she had a nervous tension in her voice.

"Jasmine, of course, you're my little sister! So why would I not be there for you and love you any less," I said looking at her like she was crazy. Her expression didn't change as she studied my eyes. It looked as if she was stalling so she could calculate her next move.

"Okay, I was wondering if..." She looked past me and out of the room. "I need to know if you..." She paused again. Her eyes darted towards the entrance of the room a second time. I turned my head and I heard my father's voice coming from downstairs. It sounded as if he was talking on his phone. I heard my grandma ask Maya to take a bag into the kitchen. I looked at Jasmine who had a startled look on her face. "I'll talk to you about it later." She jumped up and started walking towards the door. I grabbed her and stood up, turning her body so that she was facing me.

"Hey, hey, hey! Alright, that's cool, but are you going to be okay?" I smiled placing my hands on her shoulders. I dipped down a bit to look her square in the eyes.

"Yeah, I'll be fine. We'll talk about it later, okay!" She said in a hushed tone. She rushed to the bathroom. I shook my head and made my way back downstairs.

Everyone but my dad, whom was outside on the porch talking on the phone, had migrated to the dining room. I heard them talking about the hat Grandma had bought. She was trying it on as I walked up.

"So your hat is more important than hugging your grandson?" I said. I wrapped my arms around her and kissed her on the cheek. She let out a laugh as if I was tickling her.

"You lil' rascal, you. Come here. Now how you gon' fix your mouth to say that. Hey, sugah! When did you get in?" She turned to hug me and gave me a kiss on the cheek. She still looked the same; it was as if time were standing still where her age was concerned. Her skin was wrinkle free smooth and the color of almonds as well. Her eyes reveled a since of God fearing wisdom and knowledge. She had a few strands of gray scattered throughout her hair. It stopped at her shoulders and

166

was curled under. It framed her sweet face perfectly. Her stature set the stage for the women on my dad's side of the family. Short, stout, and feminine.

"I got in a couple hours ago. Hey, Mama!" I said smiling and walking over to hug my mom. My mom still looked the same as well save for a few gray hairs peaking their way through her thick jet black hair. She was wearing an up do and her smile sparkled as she stood back to look at me. She was wearing a new pair of designer eyewear and a light coat of lip-gloss covered her full lips. She had slimmed down some since I had seen her last and the rose colored blouse she was wearing complimented her skin tone very well.

"Hey, boy! How was your flight?" Mama asked. She wrapped her arms around me and gave me a quick squeeze.

"It was pretty good. Nothing to complain or brag about," I responded.

"You like your grandmama's hat?" Mama asked. Grandma struck a pose and modeled her latest purchase. It was a beautifully detailed hat with a semi wide brim, a tasteful floral arrangement on one side, a satin ribbon surrounding the dome, and it was finished in a brilliant bronze hue.

"Hmmm, let's see. Yeah, I do actually. That's really nice. I like it." I said taking a quick examination of the hat.

"Good because I picked it out." Mama said laughing. Grandma took the hat off and gently placed it in the box. She laughed a little bit and cut her eyes at my mom.

"Now LJ, your Mama said she was gon' say I picked it out if you said you didn't like it because she knows you always speak your mind." She grabbed the bag the hat came in and folded it up.

"Mama, you are a trip. You did?" I said laughing. I directed my attention towards her awaiting her response.

"You know how critical you are. So we had to put it to the test." Mama said. She gave me a cheesy smile and pulled out a chair so that she could take a seat.

"Now we both picked it out. It was the first one we saw when we walked into the store," Grandma said. "Take and put this in Grandma's room, Maya."

"Okay, Grandma," Maya said reaching for the box. "Just sit it on the bed baby." She turned towards me. "So my main man made it on in, huh?" She said. She sat down in one of the dining room chairs. "How you like being in the Navy?"

"So far I don't have any complaints. I like my job. Plus, I'm going to school and meeting all types of folk. I like it." I said. I was running through a checklist in my head of the standard series of questions I was about to be quizzed on. I thought to myself, here goes.

"You ain't gon' get caught up in all this mess with that Bin Laden character are you?" She asked. She had a look of genuine concern on her face. To keep her mind at ease, I had to give her a political answer. Because of the job I held in the Navy, it was possible that I could be called to action.

"Well, the way it's looking now, if I have to go, then I'll go. I wanted to volunteer when it happened, but I got orders and have been accepted to this school. So now I'm trying to dodge the bullet so to speak," I explained.

"Humph! The devil is so busy. We're living in Revelations, and we all got to get it right with God. I know this was a big blow to America, but it's easy to see that God is trying to give us a wakeup call," Grandma prophesized. She was staring at me intently. "I hope you don't have to go over there. It's bad enough your daddy gon' have to go over there."

"I know, Grandma. I don't think I'll be going. The unit I'm going to is non-operational. It's a training command, but I still have a designator on my record because of the training I went through while working with the Marines, so I'm praying I don't have to go now. I really want to get this degree," I said.

"I'm gonna send some prayer up too." Grandma looked up towards the ceiling and waved her hand in the air real quick like she was in church. "And speaking of prayer, you found a church out there?" she asked. She crossed her legs and adjusted the pillow in the chair she was sitting in. Just as I predicted, that was question number three on my list of what she'd ask.

"No, not yet. There is a church that I go to every now and then, but I haven't found a permanent church yet." I stayed mindful about outwardly rolling my eyes at her. I didn't want to disrespect her, especially in my dad's presence, but my inner self was huffing, puffing, and eye rolling all at the same time.

"Why not? Have you been looking for one?" she further questioned. There was that judgmental face I swear she gives me all the time. Maybe that wasn't in my head. I thought to myself, I knew I wasn't going crazy. I felt a cold sweat start to form around my neck. I unzipped my hoodie hoping that this game of "Christian Jeopardy" would end soon.

"I'll find one, Grandma," I replied hoping that would appease her for now.

"Alright. Time is winding up," she said getting up from the table. She walked into the kitchen. "Ya'll hungry? Thank God my babies made it on in. Thank you, Jesus!" I turned and saw her wave her hand in the air and quicken as if the Holy Spirit had just touched her. I chuckled under my breath.

"You know I'm hungry, Mama." My dad said as he walked in closing the front door. He had a broad smile on his face as he strutted through the entrance of the house.

"That's not surprising!" Grandma said laughing. My dad walked into the kitchen. He kissed her on the cheek. "Jason, take and bring that pitcher to the table." She instructed my Dad. "I just got to slice up this cornbread."

"AY JUNIOR! Come see about your old man." My

dad said as he walked into the dining room. He sat the pitcher on the table. We hugged each other as Grandma stood in the doorway with her hands on her hips. "Main man made it on in, Mama," he said looking at me with a look of pride. "You look good, boy. All GQ, what's that...Gucci?" he said pulling on my clothes.

"Thanks, Daddy. No, it's not even close to Gucci." I laughed. I shook my head at him.

"You're the one with all the loot." I noticed just how much I looked like him. He was a darker version of me, had more muscle mass than I did, and since he was on leave, he was rocking a goatee. He was a very handsome man who could charm the best of them.

"Oh my bad, that's that Versace. You know I can't keep up with your fashion," he laughed.

"You got jokes, I see. You been alright?" I asked playfully tapping him on the shoulder.

"Yeah, I'm fine. Just happy to see my son that's all. You alright, boy?" he asked, still visibly beaming from ear to ear.

"I'm good. I'm glad to be in the city and out of the country," I said laughing. Grandma came up and placed her hands on him and me. She whispered a quick prayer and hugged us both tightly. Aunt Rayna and Mama began bringing food to the table. My dad and I moved out of the way.

"Ya'll come on in here so we can eat!" Grandma said as she walked back into the kitchen. I ran upstairs to go and wash my hands. When I came back downstairs, everyone was ready to join hands in prayer. My dad led.

"Every head bowed and every eye closed." He joked. "Father God, we come before you humbly, yet boldly Oh God. We thank you for the many blessings you bestow upon us each and every day, Lord God. We thank you for the fellowship of family and bringing us together in your presence, Father God. Lord we ask that you keep a watch out for my brother and his family as they travel to join us. Lastly Lord, we thank you for the food we are about to receive for the nourishment of our bodies. In Jesus name, we pray. Thank God! Amen."

"Amen!" We all said in unison.

I whispered a silent prayer in my mind as I sat down. Thank you God for getting me through the first few hours of family. Grant me the blessing of not having to make an impetuous venture to Chicago ahead of schedule. Amen!

I didn't mean to, but I woke up as soon as I saw the first glimpse of light outside. I guess I wanted to hurry the days along so that I could wake up in the arms of the man I was falling for. We had an amazing conversation the night before. I was staying with my mom's mother, whom we affectionately called Granny. I had arranged this so I could visit with everyone.

She had gone to bed early the night before, so after a short conversation with her, I was immediately on the phone with Gary. I'm not sure when I had gotten off the phone with him, but I know we were up until the wee hours of the morning since Gary was working a late shift at his job. I was able to keep him up.

Shortly after waking up that last morning in Detroit, I received a phone call from my sister letting me know that she really needed to talk to me about something. I hadn't fully discussed the whole gay thing with her, but I figured that was what she wanted to address.

I felt something strange in her tone, so I went and picked her up so that we could go someplace and spend some time together. We decided to drive to Belle Isle to see the reindeer huddled together after picking up a couple of hot chocolates from Starbucks. I found a place to park and that's when it got deep.

"So what's going on with you, girl? What's wrong?" I said sipping my cocoa. I moved the seat back and got comfortable on my side of the car.

175

"What do you mean what's wrong?" Jasmine asked. She was avoiding eye contact with me, so I knew something was definitely up with her.

"What were you going to ask me or tell me a couple days ago?"

"I'm scared to ask you," she said looking down at her cocoa. She was fidgeting with the coffee stirrer.

"Jasmine, what's going on?" I said smiling. I gave her a come on you can tell me look.

"My friend didn't come to visit me," she said looking out of the window. She folded her arms and then rested her chin on her fist.

"Who? Your boyfriend? What friend?" She turned to face me with tears in her eyes.

"My friend, Jason!!!! I'm late," she said as a tear ran down her face. She wiped it away and looked back down at her cocoa.

"Oh. OH! OH WOW! I know you're not talking about your..."

"Yes!" Jasmine said interrupting me. She said it as if it took her last breath.

"Oh wow, girl. How late are you?" I asked. I was trying not to panic. I was also trying to figure out the best way to navigate my way through this situation.

"I think a month and a half. Give or take a day."

"Dang Jasmine! You alright?" I rubbed her thigh to start consoling her. "I'm scared, Jason. I don't know what to do. I was going to ask you to take me to get a pregnancy test," she said looking up at me as tears began falling from her eyes again.

"Okay, okay, okay! Don't freak out. We'll get you through this. Alright, I'll take you to get this test, but you know eventually you're going to have to tell Mama so that you can see a doctor, right?" I said trying to sound brave, but I wanted to give her some sound advice and keep her focused.

"Yeah, I know," she responded, rubbing her face and wiping away the tears.

"You two don't use protection?" I asked then I realized what I said. "You know what don't answer that. Okay, so we'll do this one step at a time. Let's just stay calm and go to a drug store. And we'll go from there? Cool?" My big brother skills kicked into high gear as I thought of ways to help alleviate some of the stress she must have felt.

"Okay," she said tearing up again."

"Stop crying, baby girl, alright? It's gonna work out for the best." I said as I hugged her. She wiped her face with a napkin.

We drove to a CVS and I made a phone call to Leyah. I asked her which one of the home tests would give us the most accurate results. She told me to buy the First Response Test, stating it may give you a false negative, but not necessarily a false positive. I went into the store and got it for her. I bought two of them to be on the safe side. The lady at the counter jokingly asked me how late I was. We shared a quick laugh. I completed the transaction and rushed back to my sister.

We couldn't necessarily go over to a family member's house because someone would be there, so we ended up going back to the Starbucks. We went over the directions on the box a couple of times before going inside. Jasmine stuffed both tests inside of her purse and walked casually to the bathroom. I sat down on one of the couches and waited anxiously. About fifteen minutes later, she emerged from the bathroom. She walked outside towards the car. I followed her and unlocked the doors.

Once we were both in the car, she removed a rolled up paper towel from her purse. Without saying a word, she unraveled the testers. Both of them displayed a pink plus. Jasmine wrapped them back up and put them back in her purse. I was stunned but excited at the thought of being an uncle.

"Wow, I'm going to be an uncle." An overwhelming feeling of joy wrapped itself around me. I thought about how wonderful it would be to have a little kid to spoil and do all of the things that my uncles and aunts did for us when we were little kids. I also saw my little sister in a whole new light. Just that quick, things changed. She was no longer my kid sister following my every move. She was a woman now. It was as if she instantly grew up before my very eyes when she emerged with the news.

"Yeah, because I'm not going to get an abortion. I don't believe in it, but I'm scared LJ. How am I going to tell Mama and Daddy?" she rhetorically asked crying and shaking.

"Come here," I said as I hugged her and rubbed her back. "Let it all out okay. It's okay. I'll be there with you, alright? I'm already in collusion so to speak. You got me out here buying pregnancy tests like I'm some broad."

"Shut up!" she said laughing and wiping her face. I was trying to usher humor into the situation however slight.

"UGH! Don't be rubbing your face after you done touched them pissy sticks." We both laughed as she pushed me. "See, we're going to look back on this and laugh again one day when we tell this story to my little niece or nephew."

"Will you be there when I tell Mama and Daddy?" She asked with concern in her voice. She was trying to pull it together. I could not imagine how scared she was or what thoughts were running through her mind.

"Yes, I will," I stated reassuringly. I definitely wanted to be by her side if she needed me. I was scared for her. I didn't feel there was an easy way to deliver this sort of news.

"Now what about this biscuit head boyfriend of yours? He'd better man up if your doctor results come back positive. He got a job?" I asked with a serious tone. I locked eyes with her, so that she understood I meant business.

"Yeah, he just started at FedEx last month," she replied.

"Oh yeah. Why you looking like that?" She had a look of bewilderment on her face.

179

"What if I have to go through this by myself?"

"Hey, worst case scenario, you got us. Mama had me when she was around your age, and she had support from Granny and them. You just make sure you finish high school by any means necessary. Do what you gotta do for you and the baby. If he's a real man, he'll stand up, Jasmine. Just be straight up with him and know that we'll have your back either way it goes okay?"

"Okay," she looked at me and smiled with what looked to be reassurance.

"This is going to be a shock to Mama and Daddy, but hey we'll get through this. But you gotta tell them Jas. That way you can get the right care."

"I know," Jasmine said realizing there was no way to avoid the inevitable.

"Now don't make this a habit lil' girl!" I smiled. "You are not one of them girls on Maury! Or are you?" I said sizing her up.

"No, stupid! God! I only did it with Khalil," she said looking down at her lap.

"So I'm not going to see you on T.V. in a couple of weeks?"

"No, Jason. I'm not one of those girls," she giggled.
"Okay."

"Let's go and get this over with," Jasmine somberly decided.

"You ready." I asked.

"Yeah, I don't have a choice. I'm still scared

though," she said.

"Well, guess what. We've been taught how to pray. So let's send a prayer up and break the news to the new grandparents."

We said a prayer and made the journey back to my Grandma's house. I was getting nervous for my sister because I was unsure what my parents' reaction would be. First, they have a gay son. Now their baby girl, who was on the fast track to college, is pregnant. I was scared for her, but deep down, I just felt that it was going to be okay.

We made it back to the house and I parked the car. Jasmine grabbed my hand and told me that she wanted to wait until they got back to Texas before she let the cat out of the bag. She said she didn't want to put a damper on the trip. I empathized and respected her decision. We got out of the car. I put my arm around her and pulled her in close to me as we walked up to the house. I let her know that her secret was safe with me, but informed her not to wait too long. Wow my baby sister is pregnant. I was not expecting that. I ain't even had sex yet, I thought to myself, is everybody fucking but me?

Windy City Here I Come

I will never forget the first time I saw the Chicago skyline. It was nighttime. The view of the city lights of downtown twinkling against the dark backdrop was extraordinary. I had just hit the Dan Ryan expressway headed to Gary's house. There was something so inviting about this city. It was as if the skyline were a pair of arms welcoming me home. I felt at peace all of a sudden like this was where I belonged. I was listening to "Act Too (Love of My Life)" by The Roots just feeling all kinds of energy radiating through my body.

I left Detroit earlier that afternoon later than I had anticipated. Gary warned me about the traffic during the day. He told me that he had to take care of some additional tasks at the station, but assured me I would definitely have his undivided attention for the duration of my stay. I followed the directions he gave me and pulled in front of the parking garage of his building. I called him to let him know that I was outside. A couple of minutes later, the gate opened and Gary emerged with a huge smile on his face. He motioned for me to drive into the garage and pointed to where he wanted me to park. Gary opened the car door as I unbuckled my seat belt. He grabbed my hand and pulled me out of the car.

"Got-damn! Bring yo' sexy ass here. What's up, baby?" he said squeezing me and lifting me off the ground. I let out a slight laugh and wrapped my arms tightly around him. I was elated to be back in his presence.

"What's going on, babe?" I said as he put me down. I passionately kissed him on the lips before he could answer my question.

"Alright, don't start anything out here boy," he laughed. "I can't be held responsible for what happens," he said as he gave my butt a firm swat.

"Really?" I smiled.

"Really!" he replied. "Come on, let's get you upstairs," he said. I popped the trunk. I grabbed my keys, phone, and put my jacket on. I walked to the back of the car to meet him. He had taken my two bags out of the car.

"Here, let me get one," I said as I shut the trunk.

"I got it," he said turning to kiss me on the forehead. I followed him to the elevator rubbing his hair. He'd cut his dreads. He now had a mini fro which was tapered. It looked pretty good on him.

"Aww what made you cut your dreads," I said rubbing the back of his hair.

"It was time for a change. Plus, I'm trying to get this promotion, so it was just something that needed to be done." he said as the elevator doors opened. We entered and he pushed three.

"I got you," I said taking in his masculine beauty. It was so good to see him. I had a combination of nervous energy and serenity struggling to gain my minds attention.

"Why you don't like it?" he asked.

"No, you look good and polished. I did like your dreads though but this works too," I said.

"So does this," he said rubbing my head slowly. I had cut my hair close and had it lined up earlier that day. It was something different in his touch this time. It was as if he was savoring that moment of contact with my skin. My body shuddered as I closed my eyes for the duration of his hand movement.

We reached his floor and walked down the hallway towards his apartment. It was an older building that looked to have been rehabbed and modernized. It was old school with crown moldings accenting the ceiling, and up-to-date light fixtures. We made it to his apartment and Gary opened the door. The aroma of Vanilla incense hit me and calmed my senses. His apartment was pretty tidy. You could tell it was a bachelor's pad though. He had the usual gadgets and toys to play with: a big television, a PlayStation, an Xbox, nice couches, and I loved the hardwood floors. He had candles lit, and some Kenny G. playing in the background. The lamp in the living room was dimly lit.

"Alright, baby, let me have your jacket, and you can make yourself at home. He paused as I removed my jacket. "And I'll take these to the room?"

"Cool." I said as he took my jacket. I reached into the pocket to remove my brush. "I like your spot," I said taking everything in.

"Yeah, this is home," he said looking into the living

room. "I hope you have a heavier coat than this?"

"Yeah, it's in my bag. I didn't think it was going to get too cold, but I brought it just in case."

"Cool. It might. This is Chicago babe, so you never know," he said hanging up my jacket. "It'll be raining one minute, snow for ten good minutes, and then be 80 degrees all in the same day babes."

"Really? That's crazy!"

"Yessir, so get ready." He closed the closet door and kissed my lips scooping me up into his arms. I gave his left bicep a peck and looked up at him and smiled. "Okay, go sit down, get comfortable, take your shoes off, and give me a minute to put your stuff up. I ordered some Thai food from this place up the street. It should still hot. I picked it up right before you got here. Cool?"

"Yeah, that's cool. You know I love Thai food!" I exclaimed.

"That's cool, but you gon' love something more than Thai food after this trip?" he said kissing me on the forehead.

"Okay, but I need to use the bathroom," I said blushing.

"Follow me," he said directing me to the bathroom.

I walked inside, and shut the door behind me. I relieved myself and walked over to the sink to wash my hands and brush my hair. I turned the water back on to drown out the sound of me opening his medicine cabinet. I was looking for HIV medication or something out of the ordinary. Hopefully, I wouldn't find out anything he said about his health was a lie. All I saw were the usual suspects. There was Tylenol, Nyquil, toothpaste, and a thermometer. I opened the bottle of Tylenol just to make sure. It checked out. I replaced the bottle and turned the water off. I took a deep breath, opened the bathroom door, and slowly walked out to the living room.

His face lit up when I entered the room. I took a pause and leaned up against the wall. He'd arranged everything as if we were in an authentic Asian Restaurant. The food was on an elevated platform with two oversized pillows on either side of it. There was a bottle of wine chilling on ice, and of course, him...in all of his sexy splendor.

"Why you standing over there?" he asked. He had a cheesy smile on his face as if he were about to laugh at any given moment. He had the lights in the room turned off. There were candles lit all around the room. There was a set of tea lights forming a heart on the floor beside the table.

"I'm just taking you in. This is really nice." I wondered what was going through his head. Was he thinking the same things that I was? How happy was he to see me? He was experienced at this. Hell, was he even nervous?

"Well, it's even nicer over here. Come here, baby," he said reaching his hand out to me. I removed my shoes and walked over towards him. I put a slight strut in my step trying to be a little manlier. I guess I thought that would counteract the emotion bubbling up inside of me. I'm sure it appeared that I was trying too hard in my attempt to pimp walk.

"How was your day?" I asked. I eased my weight down on the pillow.

"It was a blur," he said squinting his eyes.

"Why?" I asked getting comfortable. I clasped my hands together and sat Indian style as I gazed into his eyes. The dim lighting and soft scents wafting from the candles danced in rhythm around our silhouettes being cast against the wall.

"Because I was all excited about you getting here. So everything else that happened around me today was irrelevant." He smiled. I blushed and bit my lip as I looked down at my lap and slowly raised my head to look back into his eyes.

"I couldn't wait to see you, but it seemed like it took forever for this day to get here," I said. I was so thankful that this day was here.

"Yeah, something like that." He smiled. He licked his lips after his statement very seductively. "How was the family? I don't see any fresh bruises. So from the outside, it looks like you haven't been in a fight or nothing," Gary said smiling.

"No, no fights. I made it by the sweat of my brow," I said wiping my forehead. I paused and let out a nervous chuckle. I tried to gain control of the nervous ball of energy I was becoming with each moment that passed. "Everyone is fine. My grandma's party was really nice. I had a really good time tripping out with my cousins and my sister. And there was no drama, Thank God!"

"I'm glad to hear that. See, I told you not to worry. You went up there with your knives and daggers sharp as hell and didn't even need to use them." He laughed. His laugh was so sexy, and he did this little bounce when he laughed. I was really studying his every nuance and recording it someplace in my mind to draw upon, for those times when I won't be around him.

"Be quiet," I said smiling in a shy manner like a young boy.

"So are you happy to be here?" he asked winking his right eye at me.

"You can't tell," I said leaning in towards him until the tips of our noses touched. I backed away slowly as he tried to kiss me. This was my eager attempt to transfer some of this nervousness on to him and appear ready for whatever the night was to bring.

"You little dick tease. That's all right. I got you," he said shaking his head. He picked up a napkin, balled it up and threw it at me.

"I'm mad I got to be a dick tease. Punk!" I said as I caught the napkin in mid-air.

"I just call it like I see it." He smiled shrugging his shoulders. He then grabbed the wine and bottle opener and started screwing it into the cork. He gave it three good turns and pulled it loose.

"Whatever," I said as he poured some wine into my

glass. "So what do you have planned for me while I'm here? Oh and at some point I have to drive up to Great Lakes to see the base and take some paperwork to the school," I reminded him.

"I got you! And as far as recreation, I got to show you around the city of course. I have to take you to my favorite restaurant, Dixie Kitchen. It's a lil' Caribbean spot." He paused and thought for a couple of seconds. "We must do the Sears Tower." He paused again as he threw out his hands extending his fingers to continue the countdown of his list. "We might check out a club. And I definitely have to wrap you up in my arms in Boys-town." He paused again and rubbed his hands together. "But let's take care of your business first and then play it by ear. We're gonna have fun, no doubt. I got you, baby!"

"Cool. What's Boys-town?"

"That's the gay side of town. It's on the North side of the city on a street called Halstead," he said placing a napkin on his lap. I took his lead and unraveled my own. I folded it into a neat triangle and placed it over my right knee.

"Cool. I'm excited about being here." I picked up my glass. I took a long sip of wine hoping it would calm the effects of my nerves. I then took my chopsticks in hand and maneuvered some rice onto my plate.

"I'm excited about you being here too. You's a pro with them chop sticks," Gary observed.

"You don't know how to use them?" I asked trying

to seize an opportunity to teach Chopsticks 101.

"Naw, I just put them out here for decoration," he said as I laughed. I grabbed a set and handed them to Gary.

"Okay, I'm gonna show you how," I said demonstrating mine. "Put them both in your hand like you're about to write something on a piece of paper." I waited for him to position them in the first step.

"Okay. Now what?" He asked. Looking at my hands.

"Now take your middle finger and split them   like this." He followed suit. "Now your thumb and index finger are going to do all the work like this." I moved the chopsticks up and down tapping them together to demonstrate the final technique. "Your middle finger serves as the base to rest the lower stick on. See?"

"Okay I got it. Let me try this." Gary tried picking up a piece of chicken. It dropped once he had it up to his lips. He tried a couple more times. Again it dropped. I told him the secret is to bring his mouth to the chopsticks.

"I'll work on that later. I'll starve to death trying eat with these fuckers." He laughed and tossed them to the side of his plate.

"You so silly," I laughed. "Gary, you didn't even try," I said with a hint of disappointment.

"I did try. You just saw me. I'll practice later, baby." He laughed and winked at me as he stuffed a fork full of chicken into his mouth. It was even cute the way he ate. I was getting turned on just watching him do that.

191

"Are there any open mic sets we can go to?" I asked. Gary was adding more food to his plate. I took that moment to quickly adjust my slight erection while he was looking down.

"You know what? Yeah, there is. I got a set I can take you to on Friday night. Why, you gon' read something?" He smiled looking at me. He sat one of the containers back in the center of the table.

"Um, I don't know, I might." I said in a low tone. I was a little shy about reading my stuff in public. So far the only audience I had was my friends. I did want to do an open mic session eventually though.

"Let me hear something. You know any off the top of your head." he said with excitement in his voice.

"You'll just have to wait until Friday." I said trying to brush it off.

"Nope, don't be making me feel common. Make your man feel special. Spit something." he said biting into a dumpling.

"Alright, alright. Um, let me see." I said looking up at the ceiling. "I'll give you a piece of one that I'm still working on. You ready?" I smiled and placed my chopsticks on the plate.

"Go for it," he said placing his fork down.

"Okay," I said clearing my throat. So this one is untitled and it's like..."

Things familiar to us often get lost alongside our fading sight and vision of a romanticized view of the world.

God's peace surpasses all understanding for a reason, Because though we think we live this life to fulfill our own desires and purpose,

Certain moments, events, even answers are not our own.

We try desperately to keep life mental as we hold on to good times,

Like how I talk all this junk about being a poet, Get on the mic all nervous and stoic,

A true poets head will hurt sometimes with words, sounds, and ideas for prose bouncing around the head in an abstract rhythm like mix tapes

Till they bleed onto my Mead,

I just want to feed the inner realms of your being...

"End scene," I said smiling. I looked down at my plate trying not to blush.

"Oh, you gotta finish that before you leave. I want to know where you're gonna go with that," Gary said. "Good deal, baby!"

"You liked it," I said looking up at him anticipating his reply.

"Hell yeah! I loved it," he said with a look depicting the question of, are you crazy?

"Cool." I smiled. I grabbed my chopsticks and tapped my bottom lip with them.

"Have you ever done an open mic?"

"No, I want too though. I just feel like my stuff is juvenile. I'm not sure how people will take it. I've never read any of my writing to an audience."

"You're probably traumatized by your Mother reading your journal." Gary looked at me with concern and understanding in his eyes. It made me want to open up more about the subject with him.

"That could be it. I still can't believe that happened. It was some personal stuff written on those pages, baby," I said shaking my head. I continued to give him direct contact. I wanted to be completely honest with him from this point on. I found comfort in his eyes. "Do you still have it?" he asked before biting into another dumpling.

"No, I burned it in an attempt to get rid of the evidence in it. Like, I didn't want anyone else finding out about me until I wanted them to. If that makes sense?" I said hoping he'd understand.

"I feel you. What were you writing about?" Gary quizzed.

"Oh my God, all kinds of stuff." I paused for a moment of recollection. "That's when I first started writing poetry. But the thing that sticks out in my mind was the first line of the first page reading, I'm gay." I laughed out loud shaking my head. "Bam! There they were. Those two words in capital letters, I'M GAY!" I said as I did the jazz hands. "Not only that, but I was talking about dudes I had crushes on in my school,

194

wondering what it would be like to have sex with a dude." I took a deep breath recapturing all the things I said. "I was more embarrassed than anything. So I think that could have been a reason why I burned it also. To sort of burn what was supposed to be unspoken."

"So you were burning silence," Gary said nodding his head revealing his own interpretation.

"Yeah, I mean, you don't want your mom of all people to know stuff like that. It was embarrassing, especially when you haven't come to a place where you feel comfortable enough to tell them who you are. She stripped me of that right." I looked down at my plate and licked my lips. "I feel you, baby. Well, I hope you at least open up to me with your words. I would love to hear more," he said. He reached over and gently placed his fingers up to my chin to raise my head. Our eyes locked.

"Yes. I can do that." I smiled. "Cool."

"So what's up with these lil' niggas you wanted to sleep with," he said trying to sound like a serious jealous boyfriend.

"Oh my God! For real?" I said laughing. I picked up my glass and took another sip of wine.

"I'm serious. Tell me something. I know you got a Navy story or some high school encounter." He asked trying to pump me for information.

"There's nothing to tell," I said staring him in the eye.

"Bullshit!" Gary laughed. "Why not?"

"Because I've never had sex," I said directing my eyes away from his immediately after my statement.

"You telling me... you still a virgin?" he said choking on his wine.

"Yes. I've never had sex with anybody," I said bashfully. His eyes got big. He grabbed a napkin and wiped his mouth.

"Nobody?" he said. I looked up from my plate and back into his eyes. My shyness was starting to die down. The effects of the wine were taking a hold of my mind. This caused me to get more comfortable as I let my guard down. I made a mental note not to drink another glass of it. I didn't want to get drunk and mess up this meeting. "No man, nor woman, only because I'm not attracted to broads, but no," I said with urgency.

"So let me get this straight." he said clearing his throat. "If I was so lucky to have sex with you, I'd be your first?" He had a goofy smirk on his face. In my mind, I was trying to decide if he was making fun of me or not.

"Uh, pretty much," I said looking down at my plate. "Is that like, a bad thing or unbelievable or something?" I asked wondering if my virginity was a turn off for him.

"No, baby. It's not a bad thing at all," he said reassuring me. I looked him in the face. He still had that weird smirk on his face. I wanted for him to continue. "But as far as gay niggas is concerned, it is very rare that you meet a twenty-one-year-old who is still a virgin." He paused and shook his head vigorously for a couple of seconds. "I mean you got twelve and thirteen year olds having sex now days. Hell, and giving birth."

"I know right," I said with a chuckle thinking about my sister's dilemma.

"So what made you hold out this long?" He repositioned his frame on the pillow.

"Well, call me a dreamer, or hopeless romantic, but I want my first time to be with that one dude I feel is the one," I said using the hand quotes for extra emphasis. "You know? Somebody I can see myself with."

"Wow, that's what I'm talking about. Hopefully I can be the lucky guy," he said smiling broadly. I imagined he already knew he'd be that man.

"Yeah, we'll see," I said. "Damn. My baby is a virgin," he said smiling. He brought his fist up to his mouth suggesting his excitement. He shook his head vigorously again with his eyes closed. He then yelled out WOOOO!

"Now I'm really nervous and embarrassed." I was smiling so hard my cheeks were starting to hurt from that nervous smiling one does when they are put on the spot.

"You don't have to be either one of those feelings," he said with a sexy smile. He bit his lower lip.

"Subject change!" I said still blushing. I scooped up some rice and brought it up to my mouth.

"I love your dimples, baby." he said winking at me.

"Do you?" I smiled.

"Yeah, so cute!" he said leaning over to kiss me on the forehead. "So this is cool. You keep surprising me. I gotta say I've never deflowered anyone before."

"Gary! Dang! You make it sound like surgery." We both laughed. I took a drink of water.

"I know right? So you've never done anything sexually," he kept quizzing.

"I mean, I've kissed and done the whole PG-13 rated groping with clothes on. But nothing major like going all the way or going down on a dude," I said in a bashful tone. Although I was a little tense about telling him this, it was a conversation that we needed to have.

"So what do you think you'd be into?" he asked curiously.

"What do you mean, be into?" I said with a puzzled look on my face.

"Now don't go blond on me. Sexually. Meaning what do you think you'd like?" he laughed.

"Gary, I don't know," I laughed. "I guess I'd have to do the whole trial and error thing. You know? Maybe going down on a dude. Like, dick has always fascinated me," I laughed to myself as a slew of dicks I've seen in my porn collection flashed through my mind. Now I knew I was tipsy. I took a pause before making my next statement. "And I have always pictured myself on the receiving end," I said covering my face with one hand. I started laughing.

"What's so funny, baby?" he said smiling as I peeked at him through my fingers. "I'm listening to you." He was really hanging on my every word.

"I can't believe I just told you that."

"Well, you need to tell me all there is to know about you if we're going to be together. I'm trying to be your man. And now that I know you're a virgin. JACKPOT!" he said doing a reverse fist pump.

"For real Gary! Seriously?" I said laughing and throwing a fortune cookie at him. I shook my head and rolled my eyes.

"Ooh, I like that rough shit too, baby!" he said. He was so sexy to me.

"In all seriousness though. If I happen to be that lucky dude you give it up too, then yo', we gotta talk about some things you know?"

"I feel you. I just don't want to feel like that's all you want," I said looking him in the eyes hoping he'd say the right thing.

"Well, I definitely want more from you. So please don't ever think that, a'ight?" Gary said. I smiled again; it was exactly what I wanted and needed to hear.

"Okay, I'll keep that in mind. So um...what do you get into?" I said letting the wine have its way with my tongue.

"Oh, so now you're getting all bold. You really want to know Mr. Virginity?" He smiled. He nodded and rubbed his hands together like an evil villain.

"Yes, negro. I asked didn't I?" I said reaffirming my boldness.

"Jason, I'm an ass man. I love ass. And yours is nice

and healthy. I love to eat it, play with it, lick it, suck it, kiss it, and caress it. I love me some ass. I love to kiss. I love getting my dick sucked. I love to fuck. But there is a difference between fucking and lovemaking. There is a time for both. I feed off of my partner's energy to please him and to make him want me all the time. I pay attention to what he needs. If you're with me, it's not always about me. You feel me?" he said flashing a sexy smile.

"Okay. Wow! Um...I don't know what to say behind that," I said as we both laughed. At that point, my dick was rock hard. If he saw it, at that point, I didn't care. But I did move my napkin over my crotch for the sake of class.

"Just marinate on it for a while," he said sipping some wine. I stole a glance at his dick. It was pulsating through his pants. I thought to myself, Oh wow! "But no pressure and no rush. We can just take our time until we get to that point. You tell me when you're ready," he continued.

"I will...if you're the lucky guy," I said trying to stand my ground over my choices. So far he checked out as the clear choice.

"Riiiiight!" He winked.

"So what would you normally be doing if I weren't here?"

"Alright, I'll let you change the subject. I'd pretty much hang out here or with my boy Andre. But when we're talking on the phone, I'm right here in the living room laying around. Maybe playing one of my games. I usually work out at the Fire House. Or go play ball with the fellas. But I don't really do too much. It all depends on what the city has going on," he said. He held up the wine bottle to offer me more. I waved my hand to decline.

"Cool. It's pretty much the same for me. If I'm not hanging out with the crew, then I'm on the phone with you or something," I said flashing a smile.

"What's or something? Your other nigga?" Gary asked playing the jealous boyfriend. A part of me knew in my bones that a part of him was serious about that question. This yet again turned me on.

"My boy warned me about you kats with that Island blood," I said shaking my head.

"And what did your boy say?" Gary laughed. He licked his lips seductively.

"My friend says that you Caribbean guys are possessive, jealous, and crazy at times," I said recalling what Michael stated about his experience with men from the islands.

"And you believe him?" he said with a straight face.

"Prove his theory wrong." I said shrugging my shoulders. "I'm just repeating what I've heard. He's been around, so he might know a little something, something." I smiled.

"I'll see what I can do. I am a little possessive over my dude. It's my protective nature though," he said reaching over to rub my leg.

"Umm hmm. That's kind of hot," I said still turned the hell on.

"Is it?" he said biting his lip.

"Yup! I like an aggressive type of guy. I told you I'm headstrong and independent. So for me, I need someone who can deal with that. Be a take-charge type of dude. Balance me out and yoke me up at times. That's a turn on." I giggled and grabbed my glass of water for a sip.

"Oh, don't worry. I'll give you just what you need," he said pointing at me. "I'll give you just enough rope to hang yourself, then yank your lil' ass back into reality."

"Thank you, sir! I will be forever grateful," I said. I used a slave voice and clasped my hands together.

"Anytime, baby," he winked.

We finished our food and cuddled up next to one another. We lay there talking, discovering more and more about one another. We were also getting a feel of each other's body. Our senses were invigorated through the sensual art of caress. It was a beautiful night, and it felt quite natural being in his arms. I could feel my world mesh with his right there on the floor with the mellifluous tone of each love song that played. I got up to take a shower and to brush my teeth. His shower was over sized with more than enough space for a couple to indulge in some naughty activities. The warmth of the water felt almost as good as his touch. I heard the bathroom door open as Gary emerged. I guess he was reading my mind because next thing I know, he slid the shower curtain back, and stepped into the shower to join me. He wrapped his arms around me and squeezed me tight. I turned to face him looking down at his dick. My eyes slowly traced their way up his body to lock with his. He joked with me asking if I liked what I saw. I smiled and shook my head yes before licking my lips. My mouth began to rapidly moisten more than normal. I definitely wanted to taste what I just saw. He had a gorgeous dick. It was a nice golden brown just like his complexion. It was pointed in a downward slope. I was taken aback by how endowed this man was. He had a thick long shaft with a nice plump head. I could only imagine how much more it would grow.

As if this were second nature, I impatiently took it into my hands when he motioned for me to touch it. His body shuddered as I circled the shaft and caressed the head with my fingertips. Gary wrapped his hands around my waist and cupped my butt pulling me in closer to him. We began kissing and tasting one another as the water drenched our bodies. My heart began to pound as the passion began to unfold.

I let out a groan as he gently sucked and nibbled my neck. I placed my arms around him tightly cradling his head as our lips met again. He scooped me up, elevating my body, drawing me closer so that our bodies would be more in unison. I enveloped him between my legs. Our chests were pressed together as he pinned me up against the shower wall. Our kisses became wild and untamed as we lapped one another up hungrily. I could feel his dick pulse and throb next to my very own. It was as if they were kissing also while getting acquainted with one another. They were two beautiful erections overtaking one another in an erotic dance of pleasure. Rigid, full, alert, and ready.

I broke from his embrace and slid down the shower wall to rest on my knees. I grabbed a towel and built up a good lather. I looked up at him and we both smiled. He was rubbing his chest. I placed the towel at the base of his dick and worked my way down to wash his feet. I worked my way back up his right leg again washing his groin region. I then moved over to his left leg, maneuvering the towel up an over his abs and chest. I turned him around to wash his back and booty. He returned the favor, except when he reached my butt; he kissed and massaged each cheek.

We then took turns rinsing one another off. Once we were soap free, Gary shut the water off and we exited the shower to dry. We then kissed our way to the bedroom. The level of passion igniting in the shower had toned down a bit. We lay naked in each other's arms, my back against his chest. He held me as if letting me go would hurt. I felt more than a connection with him. I could feel and see the genuine emotions he exuded towards me. I felt that this must be me arriving at the cusp of love. Getting to this point was easy and natural, but how do I know if love was what I was feeling? Should I stay there? And what does one do when you get there? I always seemed to over analyze things, but with this, right here, right now, there was nothing to mull over. It was what it became. Love.

A Virgin No More

Gary nudged me and let me know that we were approaching our stop. I was hoping that I did not freeze in the jacket that I was wearing even though I had on layers. Gary had jokingly stated that I was trying to be all next level fly for him. Even if he was right, I didn't care because the excitement of exploring Chicago for the first time was flowing through my bones.

The train came to a stop. We exited and walked down the platform to street level. The sun was out, and there was a slight chilly breeze making its way through the crowd. The city was so alive. The sounds were its energized heartbeat. There were people from all walks of life out and about. It was a melting pot of ethnicities and reminded me of my trip to Paris.

Our first venture was going to be the Sears Tower. Gary told me we would be able to see the whole city. We took pictures and I marveled at the views. I was amazed at how large the city was. If Chicago is the third largest city and New York was number one, I couldn't fathom how much further it would stretch out judging from the view out of the Sears Tower. You could see for miles. Luckily it was a pretty clear day with minimal smog.

From there we walked down Michigan Avenue, better known as the Magnificent Mile. We did a little bit of shopping and headed over to the Water Tower Place to warm up and grab a bite to eat at Food Life.

Aside from all of the glamorous parts of the CHI, there were rough areas as well. We got on the train and rode for a while. I saw the Southside, and a portion of the Westside. The city was full of old buildings and Grey Stone homes with very detailed architecture. The city was very diverse and broken up into various ethnic groups. The demographics, according to Gary, changed up every few years. A lot of folk were moving further and further into the South and West suburbs.

You had Humboldt Park where most of the Puerto Ricans reside. There was Greek town, which speaks for itself. There was a very rough urban area known as K-town. The nickname came about because most of the streets in that area started with the letter K. There was the Near Northside with a large Irish population. The Southside varied depending on what part you were in. I learned that back in the day, the South side used to be where you lived if you were doing pretty well for yourself. It too was very diverse as far as Black Americans were concerned. It encompassed an area known as Hyde Park. It was a pretty cool area, with its artsy vibe and quiet atmosphere.

Then of course there was Boys-town. The gay district with its rainbow clad street lamps lighting the way to pride down Halstead Ave.

We headed back down town and ended the trip at Buckingham Fountain. It was near dusk, and the fountain was illuminated with a color pallet changing at various intervals. It was detailed with an intricate aquatic design and shooting water several feet in the air. There were numerous people posing and taking pictures in front of it. There were little children running around, and spectator's like Gary and I sitting and talking.

He told me that he used to come here and just sit and people watch. The sound of the people mixed with the soothing sounds of the water helped him to clear his mind. He hadn't been in a while because this was also the place where he and his ex- had their last conversation face to face. It seemed as though he may have still had some type of feelings for him. I felt this was due to the fact that closure had not been established. He told me that he was just now getting back to a place where he could visit the area again without feeling strange. We walked around a little and talked more before heading back to the car. We drove to the Southside to buy some wings and headed back to his place.

The next day we drove up to Great Lakes. Gary had never been to a military installation, so his head was on swivel looking at all the recruits and service members carrying out the plan of the day. We rode around Waukegan also. I wanted to take a look at the area where I would possibly be living. Michael and I hadn't figured out if we'd want to be closer to the city or closer to work. Judging from the drive and traffic, I was leaning towards being closer to work. He and the crew had called a couple of times to see if I'd come up for air. As much as I was enjoying my time, I did miss my friends.

Gary also took me to the fire station. I was able to see what he does, play with some of the equipment, try some things on, and meet some of his co-workers. It was a pretty nice experience. I didn't realize just how much went into fighting fires, with all of the preparations and safety checks they had to stay on top of.

My last night in Chicago, Gary and I had dinner over his best friend Andre's house. He and Gary grew up together on the Southside. Andre says he had always messed around. He thought Gary didn't know, and just like Gary, finally dealt with it and accepted it. Gary said he found out about Andre when they were talking about one of Andre's sexual encounters and Andre slipped and said ol' dude, instead of ol' girl. Andre in turn joked about Gary's proposal and possible marriage.

He had a beautiful house out in the south suburbs of Dolton. He invited the two of us and a guy he was dating over for dinner. Gary didn't care for the guy too much and felt that he wasn't a good look. He told me he had warned Andre about him and he felt that he was using him. Andre seemed to be a player - at least that was the vibe that I got from him. I figured he'd be fine. He was very cocky without being arrogant, which in the gay world is quite a task. I liked him though. He made you feel welcomed and was an excellent host.

After dinner we returned to Gary's place. I showered, packed, and picked out some clothes for the next day. Gary called the airline and paid to have my flight redirected to leave out of O'Hare International Airport, so that we could spend more time together. He then took his shower after playing a fighting game on the Xbox. He walked out of the bathroom and put a pair of boxers on. He jumped in the bed and stared at me as I ironed my shirt. He lit the candles on each night stand. I finished, put everything away, turned the lights off, and lay next to him. I rested my head on his chest and looked into his eyes smiling.

"You must like what you see," he said. "Yeah, I'm content." I smiled.

"It's something more in that look than contentment," he said rubbing my head.

"How you figure that?" I said climbing on top of him. I kissed his lips.

"I can tell," he said. He kissed me slipping me a little tongue. The most wonderful feeling rushed through my body at that instant. I kept my composure and straddled him.

"I'm ready," I said removing my wife beater.

"How can you be so sure?" he said holding my waste. He didn't move. He had a surprised expression written on his face.

"Because I've already fallen for you...I can feel it," I said leaning down to kiss his chest. The pace of my heart quickened.

"What you feel, baby?" He asked. His face now presented a sensuous smile.

"Love," I said looking him in the eyes.

"You love me like I love you?" he asked. I could feel him getting hard. I straddled him and raised my right hand in the air.

"I, Jason Williams, love you, Gary Larrieux," I said pledging my feelings.

"I love you too, baby. But you don't have to do this if you aren't ready." He gripped my waste as his eyes traced my body. "I don't want to, but I can definitely wait," he said running his fingertips across my chest. His touch was driving me crazy.

"I'm ready, Gary," I mouthed in silence.

"You sure baby. Don't play with me right now," he said looking serious and trying to maintain his cool at the same time. I felt his dick throbbing underneath me.

"I'm not playing," I responded looking him directly in the eyes.

He arose, and our lips met. I put my arms around him and felt his dick pulse against my butt. He flipped me over positioning himself in-between my legs. Our breathing became heavy as the rhythm of our kisses increased and intensified. Our tongues collided as we touched and groped one another.

He started kissing my neck and slowly worked his way down to my pecs. He circled my nipples with his tongue before playfully biting them. He kissed his way down my stomach and nibbled and licked my pelvic area. He kissed and played with my belly button while pulling off my shorts. He then turned me over so that I was on my stomach. I could hear him pulling his boxers off. He kissed his way up to the nape of my neck. My body shuddered as he placed all his weight onto me. His dick naturally found its way between my inner thighs. It was so thick and hard. He licked my ear and whispered that it was all about me tonight.

Gary worked his tongue down the center of my back. His strong hands were caressing my butt as he spread my cheeks apart. He slowly licked my center. He then buried his face there and proceeded to eat as if I were his main course. He held me down as I wiggled and squirmed in pleasure.

I then felt a fingertip enter me. He opened a bottle of lube, and worked his finger inside of me delicately while caressing and kissing each cheek with his free hand. He did this for a while, before placing a condom on and applying lube onto his dick.

Nervous feelings crept back into my mind as I anticipated him being inside of me. My body tensed as he lay on top of me once again. He spread my legs apart and whispered in my ear to relax and not be scared. He asked me if I was still down for this. I nodded my head yes. I tried my best to relax, as he began working the head of his dick into me. I could feel it stretch my insides as he slowly applied more pressure. He kept kissing my neck, and nibbling my ear, telling me, "I got you, baby, just relax. Let your man fill you up, baby." His voice calmed me, but I was still a little tense and apprehensive just thinking about his size.

He took his time with me and exercised an intimate level of patience. He finally got it all inside. I let out a moan suggesting pain, but pleasure as he completely buried his dick inside of me. My walls gripped it tightly as he let out a grunt releasing a deep breath and wrapping his arms around me. He held my hands, bearing all of his weight on me once again. He asked if I was okay. I replied yes. He informed me that he had filled me up. "I'm in there, baby, just relax. You feel it, Jason. Damn, I'm home. I love you, boy."

He slowly began to withdraw and thrust inward. It was uncomfortable at first and took some time to get used to it. I took him all and relaxed. He made such wonderful love to me claiming me as his own. I loved submitting to him, enjoying the fact that I was totally giving myself to him. It was an intense experience, taking us to yet another level in our newly found relationship.

We loved one another down through the night and woke up in each other's arms sticky from our night of passion. We showered and played around some more. The two of us ate breakfast, and played around a bit more before I had to leave. Gary drove me to the airport and we turned the rental car in. He helped me bring my bags to the check-in counter and walked with me to security. We hugged each other goodbye, and I told him I was going to call him as soon as I landed in North Carolina. This was definitely one of the best times I had had in a long time. I boarded my flight and

214

started to miss him already.

When I returned back home, Michael, Shawn, Preston, and I decided to go out for Pizza to catch up and talk about Chicago. We needed to plan a trip up there together, so we could all get a feel for it. It would also be another excuse to see my baby. We were still working on convincing Shawn to come with us. We nicknamed him Procrastinating Patsy because he always waits until the last minute to do most anything. It's amazing he lasted this long in the Marine Corps as much as he works on colored people's time. He is so nonchalant about everything with his old country self. In the middle of our discussion, I received a call from my mother. I excused myself from the table and walked outside to speak with her.

"Hey, lady!" I said answering the phone.

"What are you doing?" she asked. I could sense urgency in her voice.

"Right now, I'm out having dinner with some friends of mine," I replied.

"Are you sitting down?" she stated. I put my hand in my pocket.

"Mama, no I walked outside! What's going on?" I chuckled.

"Why didn't you tell me that girl was screwing?"

"Huh? What are you talking about Ma?" I asked. I was trying to play dumb hoping that she didn't already know that I knew about the situation.

"You're going be an uncle. Jasmine is pregnant!"

she blurted out.

"Are you serious?" I said trying to sound surprised.

"That's what I said isn't it? I took her fast ass to the doctor today, and sure enough she's pregnant."

"So what happened? Did she come to you or what?" I asked wondering how it all went down. The excitement of being an uncle shot through me doubly so this time because a doctor confirmed the results.

"I could just tell. She had that look about her. And when I confronted her about it, she started crying. We went to the doctor today, and the tests came back saying she was pregnant. I was so pissed. I'm not raising any more babies. And this lil' ugly ass boy she with had better man up. I just don't know what to do with the two of ya'll. This girl had a scholarship lined up and she done messed around and got pregnant. I'm too young to be a grandparent," my mom vented.

"Mama, take a breath. Are you going to be okay?" I said trying not to laugh. Listening to her rant was sort of comical. She's talking all this mess now, but as soon as the baby gets here, it's going to be a different tune coming from her. I guarantee it.

"I don't know. I'm just trying to process all of this." Mama said.

"Where she at right now?"

"She at work right now."

"What did daddy say?" I asked. I'm sure he had to be a little disappointed in her.

"I haven't talked to him yet. He still at work. You

216

need to talk to her when you get a chance. Let me get off this phone. I just wanted to give you the news. I need to go and calm my nerves."

"Alright, Ma. I'll call back later to check on you."

"Alright boy."

"Bye Mama.

"Bye," she said hanging up the phone.

I found my way back to the table and told everyone the news. I didn't want to say anything until it was confirmed by a doctor. I smiled to myself thinking about the tirade my mom just exhibited. They congratulated me and asked what she was going to do? I responded that it was her choice, but I hoped she would not do the inevitable. We left the restaurant and dropped Preston and Michael off at his place, and Shawn and I drove back to the base. I went to my room and immediately got on the phone with Gary.

"Hey, baby!" he said.

"Why can't I get you off my mind?"

"Cause you sprung," he said with confidence.

"Is that right?" I asked.

"I'm saying, come on now, it's me. How could you not be?" I could picture him hitting his chest with his palm. He did that when he was on a mission to prove validity in what he was saying.

"Ugh lame!" I laughed. "What are you doing?"

"I just got in from a game of ball. I'm all sweaty and hot. I wish you were here to take a shower with me."

"Me too. That would be really nice right now." My

mind returned to the night of our first steamy shower together. My showers have never been the same since that encounter with him.

"You in your room?"

"Yeah, I'm laying across my bed all stretched out. I got duty tomorrow," I sighed.

"What's duty?"

"More work really. Like, you see emergency patients that may come in. We stay overnight at the dental clinic in the hospital. So if someone bust their mouth open or has a broken tooth, we get them out of pain and junk."

"So, they're messing your whole weekend up, huh?"
"Not really. There ain't nothing going on out here this weekend."

"Yeah, you don't need to be in nobody's club shaking your ass anyway. I'm going to talk to your boss and make sure you have duty all the time," he joked.

"Whatever! Then I won't be able to see you either if I'm on duty all the time," I laughed.

"I'll roll through and see you. You just need to be on duty until you move here. Then I can keep tabs on you."

"Um yeah, I might need to re-think this relationship thing," I joked.

"It's too late. I got you now," he laughed and smiled through the phone.

"You got me?" It felt good to hear him say that.
"Yup! I got you. Now what?" he said.

"I don't know... Did you win your game?" I asked

changing the subject. There was a knock on my door. I got up and looked through the peephole. It was Darius.

"Naw, we lost by like ten points." He chuckled. My ankle was hurting a little bit."

"You old men always have an excuse. Hold on somebody's at my door."

"I'ma fuck you up, Jay!" he threatened.

"Yeah, yeah, yeah," I said opening the door. It had started to rain. Darius was standing there. I stepped aside and motioned for him to come in. He didn't say anything as he sat at my computer desk.

"What nigga' you sneaking into your room?"

"I'm not sneaking anybody in here. That's my homeboy."

"Um huh, let me find out."

"Let me see what's wrong with this boy. You gon' be up?" I asked. I looked over at Darius.

"Yeah, I should be, babes."

"Alright, I'll call you later." "I love you, Jay."

"Don't be testing me," I laughed.

"What you mean?" he laughed.

"Aww here you go! I know why you said that. I love you too, punk," I said.

"As long as you know..."

"Bye crazy!" I said then hanging up.

"What up, punk, long time no see!" I said looking at Darius.

"I know right, I had to go home before they ship me off. I just got back today."

"Oh yeah? What you mean ship you off?" I put my phone on the charger and lay on my bed.

"I leave for Kuwait in a couple days. I'm on R&R right now before we go to Okinawa and then head out to the dessert," he explained nonchalantly.

"Dang! Are you serious? When did you find out you were going?" I was concerned and shocked by the news because he hadn't mentioned deployment before.

"A few weeks ago... I was going to tell you earlier, but it's been so crazy. Plus, you were out of town and shit," he said playing with the mouse.

"Wow! Are you alright?"

"I guess I'll have to be. I don't know what to expect, and they trying to give us as much info as possible. They had me going with 2nd Marine Division to go into Iraq at first. And a couple days ago I got switched. So I'll be going to Kuwait to help set up a hospital, which right now, is just a Battalion Aid Station," he said sounding more relieved about his new duty assignment.

"Well, at least you'll be in a neutral and safer location. I'm hearing horror stories about Iraq from some of the guys coming back."

"Yeah, it should be cool," he said shrugging it off.

"How long will you be there?" I asked.

"Right now, they are saying anywhere from nine months to a year. This is still the first wave." The first wave of troops sent over did not have a set date and time for return. The missions were just gearing up, which meant that strategies were still in the initial stages of development as more information came down the pipeline.

"How is your family taking it? They cool with it?" I asked.

"I tried to break the news to them as best I could. Of course, they don't want me to go. They're cool for now, but my girl Donna acting a fool. She claims she pregnant now. And we ain't been together for a minute." He paused before completing his next comment. "You remember when I went home a couple months ago, right?"

"Yeah," I answered.

"Well, we fucked. She saying it ain't mine, but she ain't sure. That chick is gone in the head, my dude," he said tapping his right temple. He looked like he had a lot on his mind. I'm sure he was stressed.

"Wow! Is this the season for pregnancy or something? I just found out today my sister is pregnant?" I smiled.

"Oh yeah?" he said.

"Yup. Mama took her to the doctor today."

"Damn, but man, I don't know about this chick Jay." He shook his head.

"Man, it's going to work itself out. I know you're a good dude and will do the right thing if need be," I said trying to offer some reassurance.

"Yeah, but I got other shit on my mind. I leave next Wednesday my dude. You gon' miss me?" he asked. He tried to muster up a smile.

"Yeah, you my boy... of course I am. I'll send you care packages and junk," I smiled.

"That's cool. Don't let me get you in trouble with your man." He winked.

"Dee, I can have friends, can't I?" I chuckled.

"Yeah, but that's the thing. I was thinking..." He stopped his sentence. "Naw never mind."

"What? Now I want to know," I said trying to coax the information out of him.

"Nothing, Jay. So what you doing this weekend?" he asked changing the subject. I decided to let it go.

"Not a freakin' thing. I have duty tomorrow, so my Saturday is shot to hell. And I'm either going to go to sleep or try to make it to this one church with Michael on Sunday," I said trying to sound convincing about the latter statement.

"Yeah if I know you, you'll be at Bedside Baptist listening to the Reverend Pillow. I'm already knowing," he laughed.

"Okay! But I'm going to try and prove you wrong this time, punk," I said pointing at him. I repositioned my leg on the bed.

"So is ol' boy good for you?" he said looking at his shoe.

"I like him," I smiled.

"Sounds like you love him from what I heard, nigga." Darius said. He looked up at me. He didn't have a smile on his face.

"I mean yeah, I like him a lot," I laughed avoiding

eye contact with him.

"Well, you make sure this nigga do you right" he instructed. He had a stern look on his face when I turned back in his direction.

"I will," I smiled. He stared at me. It seemed as though he was holding back something. After a moment of awkward silence, he stood up and slid the chair under the desk.

"Well yo', I'm out. I'll holler at you later. Cool?"

"Alright. You sure you all right? Is something else on your mind?" I asked trying to make one last attempt at getting to the bottom of his feelings.

"I can't tell you that. I got to leave that alone for now," he grabbed my shoulders in his hands. He then kissed my forehead and winked at me. He headed towards the door. I followed behind him.

"Well, Dee, call me before you leave and make sure you stay in touch with me."

"No doubt. Goodnight, Jay."

He walked out into the rain towards his car. I closed the door once he got in. This was one of the most brief and weirdest interactions we'd had since knowing each other. I decided to chalk it up to him being nervous about deploying. I had a feeling of what he wanted to say. I just didn't know if I was ready to hear that type of news. Darius had to figure out what team he wanted to play on before I could be his number one draft pick. I was going to check on him later to make sure he was cool. I got back on the phone with Gary and started to iron a uniform for the next day....

What Are You Trying to Say

We were all coming into our own and growing as men, and I did the one thing that everybody told me not to do- move in with my boyfriend. I would like to think that Gary and I made a mutual decision to take the relationship to another level because I could not see the forest from the trees. We found a nice home between the base and the city. It was fairly central to his job as well as mine. I didn't have much longer in the Navy and was making provisions to discharge. I could make more money on the outside, plus the Navy was changing so much with this whole War on Terrorism happening. A lot of the jobs military members were performing were being contracted and the sea to shore rotations were becoming ridiculous. Uncle Sam wanted to keep us out to sea to increase the intimidation factor of America's naval presence while keeping Maritime trade thriving and protected during these critical economic times. Not only that, each military branch was starting to downsize like they were on the Subway diet.

In addition to downsizing, they were deploying more and more members each month. The number of individuals getting out of the service was almost equal to the number of deploying sailors, both reservist and active duty members. I was embracing the idea of enjoying my freedom and staying put for a change. I was in love not only with Gary, but also the city of Chicago. So moving again for me was not an option. If I were to re-enlist, I knew that I couldn't escape the reality of being sent to Iraq, Kuwait, or Afghanistan. Deployment times were in the range of twelve to sixteen months. Some individuals would deploy, come home for six months and then be sent right back for an additional year. I was done with my Navy career. It was fun while it lasted. Life was pretty good. Nothing left but smooth sailing, right?

Gary and I started a tradition of date night and this particular evening, kept it casual by going out to dinner, and then to the movies. For some reason, the waiter and the guy at the concession stand were both flirty and trying to gain my attention. When we got home, Gary started asking me questions with a look of concern and guilt. He was lying on the bed as I undressed. He was propped up with his hands behind his head and pillows for support watching me.

"Babe," he said. I turned toward him.

"What's wrong with you? What's on your mind?" I stopped what I was doing and laid down beside him. He caressed my cheek with his hand.

"Am I enough for you? I mean do you feel you could have or should have experienced more with..." He paused for a second and then continued. "Other niggas?"

"Where is this coming from?" I was confused and caught off guard.

"I guess the whole age thing, baby. I mean, when I met you, when I saw you, I was like that's gon' be my guy, and when we hung out that first night I knew you were the one."

"Gary, I..."

"Hold on, let me get this out," he said stopping the flow of my sentence.

"I'm sorry." I gave him a head nod and took a deep breath wondering what he would say next.

"I knew you were the one, but you're young. Babe, I got damn near ten years on you. And I have had my share of dudes." He touched my cheek. "But you haven't and I don't want you to look back one day and think you may have missed out on something. You know with different experiences, and I can't believe I'm saying this but..."

He paused again. I just continued to look at him silently awaiting him to finish his thought. I studied his face observing the conflict within him. I studied his eyes. I have never seen him look so vulnerable. I moved closer to him and placed my head on his chest. I maintained eye contact with him

"Baby, what's wrong. Talk to me," I said in a calm and soothing manner. He continued.

"I was your first, right?" he asked with a hint of skepticism in his tone.

"Oh my God! Yes! Is that what this is about?" I said offended that he'd think I'd lie about that.

"No, it's not. But you know you weren't my first?"

"Yes, I know that," I said. My eyes were still fixated on his.

"Have you ever thought about getting with other niggas?" He paused and looked up at the ceiling before looking back at me. He then proceeded. "I guess I'm asking if you feel I'm holding you back from really living out your twenties."

"Wow!" I took a deep breath. I had never thought about being with anyone else. Of course you see guys that are good looking all the time, but I would never think to cheat on him.

"Baby, I am in love with you. I love you. You know this. I can't say that I don't think other guys are attractive or anything because I'm sure you look too. I have no desire to step out on you. I want you and only you," I said tapping his chest with my index finger. "I love only you.

"I love you too, babe."

"Where is this coming from?" I asked. I felt my body tense from the uneasiness of the conversation. It was unclear where this was headed.

"You just remind me of what it used to be like when I was in my early twenties. Baby you have this spirit, this energy that keeps me young. I guess it's me tripping. When you turn thirty, your outlook on life changes. I wonder am I still gonna be desirable to you as I get older. Am I gonna be able to keep up with you and keep you on lock?" he smiled.

"Keep me on lock?" I said laughing.

"Hell yeah, that's my ass. I don't want you going nowhere, and I don't want no other nigga dicking you down or kissing you and shit. You're my dude," he said giving my butt a swat.

"You think I'm going to step out on you or something?" I asked ready to defend myself.

"Jay, it's just my insecurities rising. I see the way kats try to get at you. You're young and temptation can get the best of men sometimes," he said looking into my eyes. His eyes were darting side to side during our eye contact. I was trying to see if there was any deception there.

"So you gave in at some point? Is this your subtle way of telling me? Cause kats be trying to holler at you as well," I said with a smirk. I was serious though.

"No, no, no! It's just what I said."

"Well, you're scaring me. You sure you're okay?" I asked still studying his face. He looked away from me.

"I'm cool, babe. I just." He paused and looked back at me before he continued. "I'm about to turn thirty and shit. I got everything I want, but I just want to make sure I can keep you happy and that I'm not holding you back."

"Okay. I know how old we are, and it is what it is. I just found love early. Gary, I refuse to be some bitter jaded fag in the club falling in line with everyone else anticipating a meaningless encounter." I started glaring at him. I took a moment to think. I then got up and sat on the bed Indian style. "You know what, Gary, like I told you before. I would rather you break it off with me before you cheat on me. And if you did feel the need to cheat, you would at least respect me enough to tell me that we are missing something, or I'm not giving you what you need in our relationship. Let me know, and maybe we can fix it. But if it comes to that..." He placed his index finger over my lips.

"We're good, Jay." He closed his eyes and took a deep breath. I was trying to calm down. All types of thoughts were running through my head. I wanted to be angry. I wanted to forget about it and pretend this conversation had never happened, but I knew that was not going to be the case.

"Did you cheat on me or what?" I asked wanting to know the truth. Something about this conversation wasn't right.

"No," he smiled

"So you must want a threesome?" I asked fishing for answers and an explanation.

"Naw! Although, that would be hot," he laughed. This was his attempt to lighten the mood.

"Don't play, negro."

"Jason, we're good, babes," he reassured me.

"You want me to cheat on you or something?" I asked in a serious tone. I was starting to let go of the uncertainty I was feeling and trust that things would be okay. After all, love is supposed to conquer all. And maybe he felt that we needed to make sure that this was what we both wanted.

"You better not if you value your life." He kissed me on my forehead.

"I mean because if you're giving me a free pass, then I got to take a ride up to Evanston because your boy Josh is phyne!!!!!!!!"

"What? I'ma fuck you up!" he yelled as he started tickling me.

"Stop, STOP…. Babe! I was just playing. I WAS PLAYIN!" I said laughing.

"You better be," he said as he thrust his pelvis into mine.

"You feel that, baby?" he asked as he kissed me.

"Yeah," I wrapped my legs around him.

"Huh?"

"Yeah," I said trying to sound sexy.

"You know what I want to do?"

"What you wanna do, baby?"

"I want to wash your body."

"Do you?"

"Mmmm hmmm," he said nodding his head.

"You're so cute, Gary." I said trying to forget about what we just talked about for now.

"That's you with all the sexiness," he said tasting my lips with his tongue. His kiss reminded me of why I fell in love with him and all was right with the world yet again. Gary wouldn't do me wrong. This was real…

"Okay. Let's go shower."

"I'm sorry, baby. I didn't mean to scare you."

"Eh heh."

"Oh eh heh?"

"Um huh," I said nodding my head.

I kissed him and told him I loved him. We walked into the bathroom and showered together. He made love to me with such passion that night. It felt like he was making up for lost time -almost like he had not seen me in a while. We eventually made it to bed, and he fell asleep with his arms wrapped around my torso. His head was nestled against the side of my neck. I couldn't help but think about what he said to me that night. I wondered what really triggered this conversation. What was up with this thought he had. I took a deep look within to see if I did indeed have a desire to be with another man. I didn't feel a need to be with anyone else. Gary was all I knew. He was all I wanted. Maybe I couldn't see past that. I know some guys might not find this plausible, but it was truly how I felt. I turned toward him kissed his forehead and went to sleep. The next day was Gary's birthday. So I needed to get some rest because I had to work and tie up some loose ends before Gary's birthday party...

I woke up early that Saturday without waking Gary. I wanted to make him breakfast in bed. I had to keep it simple because I still needed to get ready for work. I prepared a meal of bacon, eggs, grits, a couple of English muffins, and some orange juice. I placed everything on a tray, and brought it up to the bedroom. I heard water running from the bathroom sink as I approached the bedroom. I placed the tray down on the bed and walked up behind him placing my arms around him

"Morning, birthday boy!" I stood on my tiptoes and kissed the back of his neck.

"Awww, you remembered. Where my present at?"

"One is on the bed."

"Oh shit, we gon' do this threesome! That's what I'm talking about," he said as he dried his hands. He turned to kiss me on the forehead.

"You know what, Gary, you always got to get nasty and take it there." I laughed. We started walking toward the bedroom.

"It's the Caribbean in me, babe. Me can't help dat all me won do is bump and grind wit me, boyfreen like BOOYAKAH! BOOYAKAH!" he said in a Jamaican accent. He wrapped his arms around me and started grinding on me.

"Come and eat, man. I made you breakfast in bed."

"My baby must love me," he said as he sat on the bed and positioned the tray over his lap.

"Yeah, somebody has too," I said giving him a cheesy smile. "Okay, so I shouldn't be long, baby. I just have a couple of patients this morning. I should be home hopefully before one, so we can trip out together today."

"So what are we doing?" he smiled.

"Oh well, I figured we could just count the gray hairs on your head. Maybe dye them. Go to Denny's for a Grand Slam and ask for the senior citizen discount. And I scheduled an appointment for a Botox treatment. OOOOH, we can also go look at Buicks'," I said laughing.

"I'ma fuck you up!" he laughed. He balled a napkin up and threw it at me.

"What? It's something about a man in a Buick Lesabre that I find so very sexy," I said. I started circling my nipples with my middle fingers. I burst into laughter.

"Take your butt to work. You are a damn fool sometimes." He laughed. I kissed him on the cheek and headed out the door. "Thanks for my breakfast, babe!"

"You're welcome, pookie wookie!"

"Stop calling me that!" he shouted. "You know you like it," I laughed.

"I hate that shit!" he yelled.

I arrived at home around one-thirty. I was on the phone between patients making sure that things were all set for Gary's party. I had a couple of my homeboys and a couple of Gary's friends bring the gifts and things to the hall I reserved for the party that night. Since it was a catered event, the caterers set the room up and decorated.

All I had to do was pretty much keep things under wraps so that Gary would be oblivious to what was going on. I told him to be ready when I got home so that we could catch a show and trip out downtown for a minute. I was able to reserve the Signature Room on the 94th floor of the John Hancock building. It was very expensive, but I had saved up for some time to make it happen.

The party was to start around 6:30. I told everyone to be ready to yell surprise and to please be on time. I was a bit nervous as to how things would look because I was not going to be able to see it beforehand. With help from his oldest sister, Wanda, I had arranged for his cousin Hannah to be at the party as well.

After the movie, I looked at my watch and saw that we had a small amount of time to kill before the party. I was really hoping that everyone would be there on time. I really wanted everything to be perfect. And I definitely wanted Gary to be surprised. I checked my phone because I felt it vibrate several times in the theatre. I had thirteen text messages and four missed calls. I read the texts and decided not to respond to them. They were basically messages saying see you there or asking questions like will there be food. One was from Wanda telling me that Hannah had made it in safely. I was   really looking forward to meeting her. I really enjoyed Gary's family. They really welcomed me with open arms. I truly developed a love for them as they did me. His sisters really took a liking to me.

I was planning the next move in my head since we had some time left. I also didn't want to get to the party right at 6:30 because I wanted to give people some extra time to make sure they would be there. So I figured I would try to have us there by 6:45. Gary went to the restroom. I decided to text Shawn, Andre, and Wanda, to let them know what time we would be there. I gave one final instruction to make sure that everyone was staged and ready. I couldn't wait. This was going to be so great. I had never done a surprise party before. So

I was really looking forward to seeing my baby's face. He came out of the bathroom and walked towards me. I felt my phone vibrate again. I took a look and there were two messages from Shawn and Andre. I replied to them to let them know that we were in route.

Gary was a little reluctant to go to the Signature Lounge for drinks, but I convinced him that we would just have one drink and go home. He was really trying to go home and watch the game. I was starting to think he would not appreciate the party. I reached the parking garage across the street from the John Hancock building. After I parked and we got out of the car, I sent texts to Shawn, Wanda, and Andre informing them that we had just parked and should be up in about five minutes or so. As we walked through the entrance of the building and headed toward security, I received a text from both Andre and Wanda. Andre's text read, "Thumbs up!" Wanda's read, "We're ready, baby!" I started to get anxious. I could not stop smiling in anticipation of what was about to happen.

We made it through security and headed through the light crowd of people towards the elevators. We rode up to the 94th floor, and he asked me why I had this big Kool-Aide grin on my face. I ended up telling him that I was just happy that he had changed his mind about coming because we had never seen the view of the city at night. He just smiled and shook his head in agreement. I could tell he was not expecting what was to come and I couldn't have been happier about it. That meant that things were going according to plan. I started to exit the elevator.

"Babe, we gotta go up one more floor," he said.

"I know. I want to get a menu real quick. Maybe we can eat here tonight."

"Jay, I'm not feeling the Signature Room for dinner tonight. If we gon' spend that kind of money, we might as well go to damn Shaw's or something," he protested. He held the elevator door open and motioned for me to get back in.

"Alright, alright, alright. But come on, real quick I just want to grab a menu and then we can go upstairs." I pretended that my phone rang on vibrate and I was answering it. I was hoping that this would irritate him. I asked him if he could go in and grab a menu for me while I took my pretend phone call. He sucked his teeth and mumbled something derogatory. He walked out of the elevator down the hall to the Signature Lounge and burst through the door. I quickly trailed behind him and heard a huge crowd of people yell out, "SURPRISE!" Immediately followed by Gary shouting in a deep frightened voice, "OH SHIT!" Everyone broke out into laughter. His sister Wanda ran up, sprinkled confetti over him, and placed a birthday boy hat on him.

"Baby, I'ma fuck you up!" He laughed while holding on to Wanda. "So this why you was on the phone all got-damned day?" he said. I laughed as he grabbed me.

"Yes, negro! I hope you like your surprise?"

"Hell yeah, this is beautiful." He was beaming. He

panned the room admiring all of the guests then back at me.

"Cool, I'm glad you're feeling it. Happy Birthday, baby!"

Hannah walked up and stood in front of him with her arms crossed. This was my first time ever seeing her. Gary talked about her on more than one occasion. He spoke of how close they were and how they used to talk about and do everything together until his parents moved the family from the Bahamas. They would occasionally hold long conversations on the phone. She told him of all the different places she had traveled and they would fill each other in on their respective lives.

She was a gorgeous woman. She had a smooth even almond complexion. Her eyes were light brown. She had thin gorgeous dark brown sister locks that were shoulder length and pulled back neatly. She was wearing a very stylish white sweater that showed off her beautiful décolleté, a pair of indigo skinny jeans which complemented her figure perfectly, and a pair of silver pointy toe heels. She seemed very girly like Gary's sisters. She was a very classy lady.

"COUSIN?!?!?!?" Gary shouted. He let me go when he realized who she was. He grabbed and hugged her so hard I thought he was going to snap her in half.

"Yeah, it's me! Happy Birthday, Gary," she said with a slight Caribbean accent.

"Girl, you look so good. How are you beautiful?" He was staring at her like she was the one toy you dreamed about opening up on Christmas day.

"I'm fine. You don't look too bad yourself," she said. He turned towards me with tears of joy welling up in his eyes.

"Jay, was this your idea to bring Hannah out here?"

"I had some help babe," I said as he grabbed me and hugged me just as tight as he did Hannah.

"Ya'll see how much my baby loves me? I haven't seen Hannah in like what...five years?" he said as he looked towards her. He hugged her again. "Yo', I am so glad that you all made it to my party that I didn't know about. I don't know how ya'll kept this a secret cause you know I keep my hand in everything, but Jay slipped this one right past me."

"I had help from Wanda, Andre, and Shawn," I piped in.

"He put it together, Gary. All I did was contact and pick up Hannah."

"Well I am grateful for the surprise. So let's get this party crackin'. Come here, baby. Thank you so much. I love you, boy," he said wrapping his arms around me. He kissed my forehead.

"I love you too."

"Babe, this is my cousin Hannah of course. Hannah, Jason. This my baby right here."

"It's nice to finally meet you. How was your trip?"

"It was fine, thank you for asking. Gary talks about you all the time. I feel like I know you, Jason," she replied with sincerity.

"The feeling is mutual. I had to at least try to get you out here. Gary mentioned how you two always miss each other during family functions and things of that nature. Not to mention how close you two were." I smiled and gave her a hug.

"Yeah, a lot of it has to do with me. I can tell you all about it later though, this is Gary's night," she said looking at him.

"Cool. Well, Hannah, I am going to mingle and make sure that what I asked for is done. I will leave you two to talk," I said. She put her arm around Gary.

"Okay. If you dance you need to save me one, so I can make my cousin jealous." She said as she looked up at Gary.

"Hey, hey, ay now. Don't come out here startin' trouble woman," Gary said.

"No problem Hannah I got you," I winked. "I'll be back," I laughed as I walked away.

People were starting to walk up and wish Gary a happy birthday. I made my rounds to thank everyone for coming and saw Andre walking around with the camcorder filming the party. He was interviewing various guests. I found Shawn and decided to formally introduce them.

"Come here, whore. Let's make this love connection happen."

"No, whore. I'm not ready to talk to him yet."

"Boy, come on here boy." I said. I grabbed his arm and we made our way over to him.

"I'm coming hag!"

"We're ready for our close up, Mr. Director," I said. I saw Shawn standing there with this nervous smile on his face.

"What's up, Jay? How you doing, baby boy?" he asked. He hugged me.

"I'm good. I just wanted to thank you for your help today. I truly appreciate it."

"Aw, no problem. You know that's my dude. You're welcome, man."

"Okay cool. So if you need a favor someday, just ask." I said.

"Well you can finally introduce me to this beautiful brother to your left."

"Oh. Well, I'll let ya'll do that. Hark, I hear the sound of a party." I hit Shawn on the butt. "Get your life baby!" I laughed and made my exit. Shawn rolled his eyes. Andre laughed. The two of them began to talk.

I was on my way to link back up with Gary, when this dude walked up to me and handed me a present. It was more than likely a CD of some sort. I didn't recognize the guy at all. I assumed maybe it was someone Gary and Andre knew. He was a slim built brown skinned man. He looked to be around my age, maybe older, and he was my height. He had a slight rugged bohemian appearance. He was attractive and had a slight Caribbean accent.

"Hey. I just wanted to say hello and introduce myself. I'm Desjardan. I'm an old friend of Gary's. I take

243

it you are his boyfriend?"

"Yeah, but don't tell anybody," I smiled. "My name is Jason, man. Nice to meet you." I extended my hand out to him. He shook it and smiled. His name sounded vaguely familiar, but I couldn't figure out why.

"I wanted to give this to you. Just a little DVD I put together I think he'll like."

"Oh okay. You could have put it on the table man with the rest of the gifts." I thought it was pretty strange that he insisted on putting it in my care.

"Oh no. I didn't see the table. I'm sorry," he laughed. "Well, I'm sure with you it'll be in good hands. Can you give it to him for me? I've got to leave." I thought to myself, you didn't see that big table in the front of the room with all the gifts.

"Okay, well, are you going to say hi to him or wish him a happy birthday? At least stay until he cuts his cake," I said looking at my watch. I was still trying to figure out why he seemed so familiar...

"I already talked to him. I just forgot to give this to him. We kind of had a falling..." The conversation was interrupted by Gary's friend Josh. They worked together at the Fire Dept. He was tall dark skinned, had a clean shaven bald head, nice strong muscular build, and a bright smile framed by a light beard. He was gorgeous. I would joke with Gary every now and then, saying that if I wasn't with him, I'd be all over him. Gary suspected that he liked me, but neither of us would dare go there.

"I'm sorry, but I have to give this brotha a hug and

say hi," he said as he embraced me like he was trying to fuse the two of our bodies together.

"What's going on, Josh? Thank you for coming," I said with a radiant smile.

"Hey, thanks, Jason. It was nice meeting you man," Desjardan said as he rushed away. I thought our interaction with one another was very odd. I paid it no mind as I slid the present into the pocket of my vest.

"Okay, nice meeting you," I said as I turned towards him to speak. "So what's up boy? What you been up too?"

"Nothing much. Just doing me. Yo', I didn't mean to run your friend off," Josh said motioning towards Desjardin.

"Oh naw. I just met him. He said he was an old friend of Gary's. You know him?" I asked trying to see if Josh could help me figure out the missing link.

"Really? Can't say that I do," he said rubbing his forehead.

"Well it is what it is. His name sounded familiar though," I said taking my mind off of it.

"Excuse me, Mr. Williams," interrupted the manager catering the event.

"Hi. How are you?" I asked.

"Wonderful. I hope everything is to your liking?"

"Yes, I am pretty happy about everything," I said panning the room

"Great. I am glad to hear that sir. Sorry to interrupt you, but you asked me to find you around this time for the cake cutting."

"Oh yeah. Okay, let's do it. Let me go find this man, and we'll be over there shortly," I said as I looked around.

"No problem."

"Come on, Josh, help me find this man. Where the hell could he be?"

"A'ight baby boy."

Sex, Lies, and Videotape

The party went pretty well. I'm very sedulous about the majority of things I plan and do, so I was very pleased at the outcome. I was also very happy to see that everyone came together to wish him well on his birthday. There was plenty of food, dancing, jokes, laughter, and the DJ was really good. I was amazed at the number of gifts he received. A couple of them were gag gifts. One in particular was a huge jar of blue M&M's. It had a huge white label with black bold letters that read: VIAGRA.

We loaded the car with everything, said our goodbyes, and made our way home. Gary let me know how much he appreciated everything and thanked me for reuniting him with his cousin. I told him it was very nice to meet her. I was looking forward to seeing her tomorrow. His family was going to get together at his mother's house that Sunday before Hannah left on her next excursion.

We reached the house and brought everything inside. It was late, so I decided I would put the things away in the morning. Gary immediately went into the living room to watch the game. He was slouched on the couch with the jar of M&M's next to him. I walked into the living room, rubbed his head, and kissed him on the cheek. I told him I was about to take a shower. He shook his head with a smile on his face.

I walked upstairs and started to get undressed. I

reached in the pocket of my vest and pulled the disc out. It was wrapped in blue Happy Birthday paper. I placed it on the bed and tossed my clothes in the hamper. I noticed that my throat was sore and becoming a little scratchy. I figured it was because of the weather. I walked into the bathroom and turned on the shower. I opened my mouth to look at my throat, and noticed some reddening, but no pustules. I brushed my teeth, gargled with some Listerine, and jumped in the shower. I dried off and entered into the bedroom at the same time Gary did. I walked over to the dresser, opened a drawer, and grabbed a pair of boxer briefs. Gary walked up behind me and kissed the back of my neck.

"What's this, babe, you made me a lovemaking CD or something?" he said. He was holding the gift the stranger left with me.

"Oh, no. That's not from me."

"Uh huh, well who is it from then?"

"One of your pieces, I guess," I smiled. "I'ma fuck you up!" he chuckled.

"This dude named um...Dejuan...no Desjardan walked up and gave it to me to give to you. I asked him why he couldn't just give it to you, but he kind of got all weird. I was like whatever. He said he was an old friend of yours," I said. Gary had this puzzled yet startled look on his face. I sat on the bed and started applying lotion to my body.

"Desjardin huh?" he said as he unwrapped it.

250

"Yeah, I think he said it was a DVD he made especially for you," I smiled.

"Let me see what this shit is."

"Yeah, I wanna know too. Pop it in," I said.

He turned the TV and DVD player on. He placed the disc onto the carousel, pressed play, and sat on the edge of the bed. I turned to face the television still applying lotion. There was a close up of Desjardin's face on the screen. He began talking.

"Hi Gary, I just wanted to wish you a very special birthday. I hope that you get every single solitary thing you deserve. You are so worth it. I figured I would take you down memory lane for a brief moment. Here is a little preview of some things you could be enjoying. I hope you're alone."

The screen went black, and then a date flashed across the screen. I scratched my head and looked at Gary. He was staring at the screen intently. After the date stopped flashing, the next image was a shot of a bed. You could hear two men engaged in conversation. I made out Gary's voice. The next image was wait...Desjardin!?!?, the guy from the party?!?! leading Gary by the hand to the bed. I looked at Gary and he lowered his head with his eyes closed. I turned back to look at the screen and saw Desjardin giving him head. Gary's face was clear as day. And I knew that the film was recent, because he was wearing a shirt that I had bought him last month. I got off of the bed and walked over towards the television to make sure that my eyes

251

were not deceiving me and my mind was not playing tricks on me. Sure enough it was Gary!?!?!?!?!...Plain as day, live and in the flesh, enjoying some head from some random ass dude...

"Gary, what the hell! "ARE YOU SERIOUS RIGHT NOW?!?!?"

"Baby!!!!" he said as he let out a deep exhale. My heart was racing!

"Wow, so this is what you were preparing me for the other night when you asked me all of those bullshit questions? ARE YOU REALLY PUTTING YOURSELF   OUT THERE LIKE THAT? HUH?" I yelled as I tried to control my breathing.

"Baby!!!!"

"NO!! Use my real name. Don't try to sugarcoat nothing. I can't even believe this...you...WOW!" He reached out for my hands. I pulled away, and walked towards the closet and grabbed a pair of jeans. He started walking towards me.

"Jay, all I can do is apologize! I didn't mean for it to happen! I just have been thinking all kind of crazy shit! This was the only time some shit like this has happened baby...just hear me out!" he pleaded. I just looked right through him.

As he was saying all this, I was buttoning up my jeans and slipping on a pair of shoes. I stopped moving as I noticed the screen. I saw Desjardin bent over the bed, and Gary behind him going to town. The messed up part about it was he was busting this nigga down raw! There wasn't a condom in sight. All I could hear echoing in my ears was Desjardin's moans and groans of pure ecstasy and pleasure. Gary noticed that I was looking at the screen and rushed over and hit the power button on the television. "Jay, I'm sorry!" he said as he walked towards me again. I didn't respond. I threw my hands up and walked around him making my way towards the nightstand. I snatched my phone off of the charger and grabbed my wallet and slipped it into the back pocket of my jeans. I was breathing heavily at this point, and pumped full of adrenaline. I was trying to walk past him to leave the room. I needed to make my way downstairs to the garage.

"Baby, say something PLEASE! At least look at me! Can we talk about this shit and sort it out!?!?!?" he said as he grabbed my arm. He yanked me back towards him just as I made it to the doorway of the room. I looked down at his hand gripping my forearm.

"If you don't get the hell off of me, dude. LET MY ARM GO!!" I barked.

"NOT UNTIL YOU AT LEAST SIT DOWN AND FUCKING HEAR ME OUT! Where you going anyway, baby?" I continued looking at his hand digging into my arm. His yelling and him questioning my next move made me even more livid. I used all of my strength to yank myself free from his tight grip. I then pushed him to the floor. I couldn't bring myself to look at him. Once free, I ran out of the room down the stairs towards the coat closet. I flung the door open, and grabbed the first coat I could find. I saw Gary coming towards me again.

"Leave me the hell alone! Run back to your other nigga!" I was struggling trying to put the coat on. I was shaking pretty bad from the adrenaline rush. I walked towards the kitchen as he grabbed me again. I yanked away and tripped opening the door. My cell phone flew out of my hand and hit the floor of the garage. I hit the button to open the garage door, reached down to grab my phone, and fumbled with the key fob to push the button to unlock the car.

"Jay, you don't have to go babe, just hear me out."

"Shut the hell up! I don't want to hear nothing you got to say. Get away from me, Gary! Running around town cheating. You should have told me that I wasn't giving you what you needed. But you punked out and fucked some other nigga! ON FILM!" I yelled.

I got inside of the car and fumbled with the key again. I was frantically trying to get the key into the ignition. I was so upset I was shaking and couldn't see straight. I tossed my coat over on the passenger side and got the car started. Gary opened the car door.

"I love you, baby. I didn't mean to hurt you. Baby, please let me talk to you. I apologize, baby!" He yelled. I looked him straight in the eyes glaring at him.

"You and your apology can go straight to hell!" I said

I slammed the door, pressed the clutch, threw the car in reverse, and peeled out of the garage and driveway. I slammed on the brakes once out of the driveway, hit the lights, and burned rubber down the street.

I just drove aimlessly. It was cold in the car, but I didn't notice until I turned the heat on. I realized I didn't have on a shirt. I just had on a pair of jeans, and a pair of shoes. I ended up in Kenosha, Wisconsin. I didn't realize I had driven that far. On a good day, Kenosha was an   hour drive north of Chicago. I managed to make it there in thirty-five minutes or so.

I pulled over and put my coat on. I looked at the clock and it read 1:17 a.m. I grabbed my phone and saw that it was off. I didn't remember turning it off. My mind flashed back to it falling on the garage floor. I hit the power button and it did not respond. I then realized that the battery was missing. I threw it in the seat. I had an emergency pre-paid phone in the console. I grabbed it and turned it on. I called Shawn and got no answer. I made two more attempts and still received no answer. I left a message for him to call me back. I put my head on the headrest and contemplated my next move. My phone rang, and it was Shawn.

"Chile, what do you want whore, I'm on sort of a date," he said in a hushed voice.

"I broke up with Gary."

"Chile cheese. You're lying," he laughed.

"I'm serious, Shawn." I said trying to make sure I sounded convincing.

"Jason, are you for real, whore?" he asked in disbelief.

"Yes," I replied with a dry tone.

"AH LORD! Shut the hell up! What happened?"

"Boy, it's a long story," I said leaning back in the seat. "Where are you at?"

"I think I'm somewhere in Kenosha."

"Chile, what the hell you doing all the way in Kenosha?" "I just started driving, and I guess this is where I ended up?"

"Ah Lord. Chile, what are you going to do?"

"Well, I don't know. I know I need to clear my head and talk. Are you at home?"

"No. I'm with Andre. I'm at his house, but you can go to my place. You got a key. I will see you there."

"I'm on the way hag. Bye."

"Jason?"

"What?"

"You alright."

I took a moment to think about his question. "No. I'm not."

"Well, know that your judies are here for you. I'll see you in a bit."

"Okay."

"Bye cunt."

I pulled up to a gas station and filled up. All kinds of thoughts rushed through my head. What stuck out in my mind most was the conversation that we had Friday night. I could not believe that he cheated. What I thought was a wonderful, loving, and thriving relationship had turned into a nightmare. I wondered what went wrong. What made him do what he did? I also thought about all the guys that I turned down. I could not see myself stepping out on him like that. I was happy with only him.

The scenes from the video replayed in my mind. I could not get the images out of my head. I couldn't get Desjardin's moans and groans of ecstasy out of my head. What further pissed me off was the audacity this fool had to walk up to me and hand-deliver the evidence of infidelity to me with a smile. Shady, heartless faggot! I felt so foolish. Then not only did Gary cheat, he fucked this dude raw. I felt like he lied to me all this time. How long had this been going on? How long would this have gone on had this video not surfaced? Was I stupid in love and so blind that I missed the signs? I could not stop my mind from approaching different angles of justification.

I finally made it to Shawn's house. I noticed Michael's car across the street as I made my way to the entrance. The last thing I wanted to do was be quizzed on the ins and outs of tonight's events. It seemed impossible for me to put on a brave face as I walked through the foyer of Shawn's building. There was a boisterous conversation creeping from the inside of the apartment. I stuck my key into the lock, when suddenly the door flew open. Michael appeared from behind it, almost breaking my key and wrist with his forceful opening.

"Bitch, you alright? Do we need to ride on this

muthafucka? Right now!" Michael said. He pulled me inside and continued his soapbox tirade. "You Northern bitches need to take a lesson from the dirty south. See we beat asses and ask questions later. What you wanna do, shit? I'm ready!"

"Oh my God! Shawn, you went and got this ho riled up?" I said rolling my eyes. I looked around and all three of my best friends were there.

"Chile, you know I can't hold water," he said as he shrugged his shoulders. "And you know once I tell Michael about some drama, he runs with it. He's the one that went and picked Preston up," Shawn said.

"Are you okay, sweetie?" Preston asked.

"Yes, boy. Hell, you know me. Jason is gon' be a'ight," I said. I faked a smile and removed my coat.

"Bitch, are you...what the fuck?" Michael said. He started to laugh. "Did you just come from seeing a bust down? Where is your damn shirt?"

"OKAY!" Preston asked as he and Shawn laughed.

"I need to borrow one. I was so mad that I only thought to put on jeans I guess. I was just trying to get the hell up out of there," I said shaking my head. I placed my coat on the arm of a chair.

"Awww, I'm so sorry, Jason." Preston said as he hugged me. I went and sat on the couch. Shawn left the room and came back with a T-shirt and a bottle of water. I slipped the shirt on and twisted the cap off of the bottle.

"So what's the deal, dish the tea! What do you

mean you broke up with Gary? What happened, because ya'll two are like...um...the gay Will and Jada or some tea," Shawn said snapping his fingers. They all laughed. I took a deep breath and shook my head. I looked up at the ceiling as tears welled up in my eyes.

"He cheated." At that point I lost it and started sobbing. Saying it out loud made it that much more real than seeing it on tape.

The Results Are In

I woke up slightly disoriented in the fetal position. I opened my eyes wide, and squinted from the light coming through the window. I looked around for a second and then got up to close the blinds. I stretched, got back in the bed, and pulled the blanket back over my body. I curled back up into a slight fetal position. I remembered that I was over Shawn's house, and the reason why came back to mind. I felt like crying but couldn't bring myself to do so. I felt like calling and cursing Gary out but didn't have the energy. I felt like shoving a pool stick so far up his ass that it would split his heart in two. Maybe that way he could feel the pain that I felt. I wanted so many things to happen, but I honestly did not want to move from the spot I was in. I could feel a rage boiling up inside of me. On top of that I felt sick. I was hoping I wasn't coming down with something. My throat was scratchy, sore, and irritated. I heard Shawn humming and walking down the hallway. A few seconds later, I averted my eyes to the doorway and observed Shawn peeking in.

"Hey!" he said in a chipper voice. The last thing I wanted was to be bothered. He walked in and sat on the bed. I slid back against the wall clutching the blanket covering me.

"You feel okay?" He asked. "Dude I don't know what I feel."

"Do you need anything?"

261

"A gun, perhaps?" I said. I covered my mouth to cough.

"Chile, no you don't need a gun. I was talking about food, or water, juice, coffee?"

"No, I just really want to be left alone for a while. I don't feel good either."

"What's wrong?"

"Something with my throat. I might have to go and get it checked out. It hurts a little bit. You got some cough drops?"

"Ahhh, I think. Let me go check."

He walked out of the room and headed down the hallway. I was thinking to myself how much I did not want to play the question and answer game today. I made up my mind to go over to the house and gather some of my clothes. I was definitely checking into a hotel somewhere for a little solitude. I needed my phone also. Shawn came back into the room.

"I'm sorry, child, I thought I had some, but I don't," he said. I sucked my teeth.

"I'll just get some later." I grumbled.

"Well. Hag. I'm about to go to the temple. I'm going to say a prayer for you, okay?" he said. I just shook my head yes. "I'll see you later. I'm not going to be long, okay?" Once again I shook my head yes. "Alright Jay, I love ya, cunt. Me and the Judy's will see you later."

I just looked at him and nodded. He walked out of the room and closed the door behind him. I heard him grab his keys and walk out the front door. I waited about five minutes and got up out of the bed. I noticed the time as I made the bed. It was fairly early. I walked to the bathroom, relieved myself, and washed my hands. I finally looked at myself in the mirror and noticed my face was void of any emotion. I stared at myself for a few minutes before going to grab a fresh face towel. I wet It with hot water and washed my face. I found a new toothbrush in a drawer and brushed my teeth. I then took a look at my throat, and noticed it was very red and had two white pustules' forming. I walked into the kitchen and gargled with some warm salt water to soothe my throat. I thought to myself, Great now I'm sick. I made a mental note to see a doctor if I felt any worse.

I walked into the living room and sat on the couch. I placed my face in my hands and sat there feeling like someone close to me had just died. It was an unnerving feeling. I got up and walked back to the room to grab my things. I walked out of the apartment, locked the door, and headed to my car. There was a light drizzle coating the city. The calm gray sky matched my mood perfectly. I reached my car and contemplated not going to the house just yet. It was still early and I didn't want to run into Gary. There was no telling what I might end up doing if he said anything to me. Michael had filled my head with all kinds of vindictive suggestions last night. I decided to go and find a hotel room in an effort to stall a little longer.

I found an Internet café in Boys-town. I signed the

register at the desk, sat down at a computer, and logged onto Expedia.com. I found a moderately priced room at a Marriot Courtyard and booked the room for a week. I figured I'd just lay low for a while. I left the café and went to check in at the hotel before making my way to the house. I drove down our street slowly until I reached the house.

I stopped directly in front of it and pressed the garage door opener. I was relieved when I didn't see Gary's truck parked in the garage. I put the car in reverse and backed into the driveway. I got out and quickly ran inside. It felt as though I was committing a crime. Once upstairs, I grabbed a large suitcase from the office closet. I quickly walked into the bedroom and started cramming it with clothes, underwear, shoes, belts, and accessories. I walked into the bathroom and grabbed my travel hygiene kit from one of the drawers, adding it to the items I had packed. I snatched my phone charger out of the socket, and threw it into the bag. I then remembered that I needed to find the battery to my phone. I walked downstairs to the garage to see if it was still on the floor, when I noticed it sitting on the kitchen counter. I grabbed it and stuffed it into my pocket.

I opened the refrigerator, grabbed a Gatorade, and walked back upstairs to grab my suitcase. I paused for a brief moment to think of anything else I might need. I noticed my laptop case next to the door. I checked to see if the computer was inside. It was, so I slung it over my shoulder and wheeled the suitcase downstairs to the car. I placed everything in the trunk, and ran back into the house to grab another coat and a jacket. I pulled the door closed behind me and walked back to the car. I pressed the garage door opener to close the door and reached into my pocket to grab the battery for my phone. I connected it and hit the power button. I sat in the driveway for a minute in a trance when the phone rang. It was Shawn. I hit ignore and sent his call to voicemail. I didn't want to talk or deal with anyone just yet. I thought about calling my boss to tell him that I would not be able to make it in on Monday, but remembered that I had already taken the next couple of days off. I made a mental note to go to see my doctor to find out what was wrong with my throat because it seemed to be getting worse.

I headed back to the hotel and took a long hot shower. Once I finished, I grabbed my phone and lay across the bed. I opened a throat lozenge and proceeded to check my messages. I held the number 1 down until the voicemail connected and then placed my Bluetooth on my ear.

"You have 27 new messages. To listen to…" I pressed 4.

"First message from, Gary, received Saturday November 17th, at, 11:47 pm. 'Baby, I know…I know I fucked up. I do not even understand my own logic for doing what I did. I didn't think I had it in me to hurt my baby. I…I want you, Jay; I want us to work through this.

Please come home, baby so we can talk...I love you so much, babe...I love you so much...Come home..." Message erased. "Next message from Gary, received Sunday November 18th, at, 12:13 am. "Jay, I hope you got my last message. Baby, I don't want to keep talking to your voicemail. I want to apologize to you face to face and get you back in my world. Just give..." Message erased, Next message from phone number 312-555-5525, received Sunday November 18th at, 12:18 am. "Hey, Jason, this is Wanda. I just wanted to let ya'll know that the family will be meeting at Mama's house tomorrow after church. So I think we'll be there around 1:30. We're going to the early service. Tell my brother because he never checks his voicemail. Thank you, see you tomorrow, sweetie." To erase press 7. To return...Next message from, Gary. Recei...Next message from, Gary'...

It seemed as if I was never going to stop pushing the number 7. I didn't want to talk to him just yet. If I did, what would I say? My thoughts kept me in a fervent mind frame recalling the video. That was my dick that he was giving to some other kat. He broke our trust and our spiritual bond of being one. The man who belonged to me gave himself freely to some other kat like it was nothing. Was it that easy? I mean what thoughts were going through his head? Did he feel guilty? Was he stroking him with the same intensity he does with me? Did he hold him ever so tightly from behind with the same level of possession as he did me? Did he kiss and nibble on that hoes ear like he does mine? Hell, did he kiss him with the same loving passion that he does me? Where the hell was my baby's head at during this? Oh my God! I lost my man, my friend, my partner, and my lover. Why is this happening?

My next thought hit me like a blow to the chest. My heart started beating faster as the name became all too familiar to me. DESJARDIN! That was his ex. Wow! A conversation that Gary and I had a long time ago came to mind, where we disclosed information of our pasts. Desjardin was one of the first guys Gary fell in love with when he started messing with guys exclusively. They had been seeing each other for a little over two years, and according to Gary, when he suggested that they become a true live in committed couple, Desjardin got ghost. Gary said that he didn't hear anything from him at all. He explained how much that hurt him. That event turned him into this cold-hearted whorish dog. He said he saw something in me that he hadn't seen in other guys to include Desjardin. I felt he still had love in his heart for him. You never get over your first love. On some level, you will always love them. But damn, did he have to take it this far?

I started to doze off when I heard Ashanti's song, 'Baby', blasting from my phone. That was Gary's ring tone. I picked the phone up and stared at his name and picture on the screen. I was debating on pushing talk when the phone stopped ringing. I laid the phone down, took a glance at the clock on the nightstand, when my phone beeped. I had received three text messages. One from Michael that read: "Bitch where are you? You better not be sitting in a tub full of hot bloody water! Holla!" The next one was from Shawn that read: "Jay we're worried about you, give me a call please." And the last one was from Gary that read: "Baby, come home so we can talk and work this out. I'm missing the shit out of you right now. I love you. I hope I still mean something to you. Come home." I hit the reply option for Gary's text and typed the word: "NO!" He text me back immediately: "Okay, I'll come to you. Where you at?" I didn't   respond. A couple minutes later he text me again, followed by a phone call. I ignored both of them.

I got up and drew the curtains closed. I hopped in bed under the covers and placed my ear buds in. I hit shuffle on my iPod and let the softness of the bedding comfort me. I figured maybe the music would take my mind off of things. But wouldn't you know it, the first song to play was "Liar, Liar" by LaTosha Scott. As I listened to the words, I placed a pillow between my legs and curled into the fetal position. Tears began to fall. They quickly soaked the pillowcase. I couldn't believe how bad this hurt.

I woke up early the next morning feeling pretty lousy. My body was damp with sweat. My throat was still bothering me and I felt sluggish. At this point, I knew I was coming down with something. I forced myself up and took another hot shower. Getting dressed was a chore, but I took my time getting ready so that I wouldn't look like a complete bum. I made my way to the north side of the city to visit my doctor. When I reached the receptionist, I feigned a smile and told her that I really needed to see Dr. Henderson. She asked for my insurance card and had me fill out some forms. She then took my vital signs and told me to have a seat. When I returned to the waiting room, I focused my attention on the television. For some reason, they had the Jerry Springer show playing. A quick glance at the title read, "Obese Cheating Lesbian Lovers caught on Tape." One couldn't help but chuckle and wonder, who comes up with this crap? The show did offer a period of distraction from my own drama, until I was called into the doctor's office.

"Good morning, Mr. Williams!" The nurse's assistant said as she ushered me to an examining room.

"Good morning."

"Please feel free to hang your coat and scarf on the door. You have a seat here. Make yourself comfortable, and Dr. Henderson will be with you shortly. Do you have any concerns or questions for me?" she said. She pulled my medical chart up on the computer screen.

"No, not at the moment," I said thinking, can you just get the doctor up in here, fish?

"Okay great, well I won't be too far away if you need anything. My name is Kelsey."

"Alright, thank you," she walked out of the office and a few minutes later Dr. Henderson walked into the room.

"Jason, good morning!"

"Hello, Doc. How are you doing?"

"Oh nothing to complain or brag about." He smiled and adjusted his glasses. He placed an expensive looking silver pen in his pocket.

"That's good," I said trying to stay within the realm of polite conversation.

"Okay, now on to business. You're a picture of health. I thought I'd only see you for your check-ups and flu shots. What brings you in today?"

"Well, sir, I don't get sick, except for the occasional cold." He adjusted his glasses, then got up to wash his hands. He rinsed them, dried them, and put on a pair of latex gloves. He walked back over towards me making direct eye contact with me. "Well, I feel pretty weak and weird. My throat is killing me. It's sore and inflamed," I said trying to recall everything I was experiencing.

"Okay, let's take a look," he said. He reached for his penlight and grabbed a tongue depressor. "Open up, and move your tongue forward. Okay, let's see something. He threw away the tongue depressor and grabbed an otoscope. "Open up again for me." He paused and I waited with my mouth agape as he examined my throat. "Um huh, Jason, how long have you had this irritation?"

"I first noticed a little scratchiness on Friday morning...maybe late Thursday night." I was getting a little anxious. I clasped my hands together tightly and tried not to fidget.

"Any nausea or headaches?" he asked.

"No headaches, but this morning I was feeling like I needed to vomit. And last night I was a little nauseous."

"Okay, I'm hoping it's not what I think it is. From your chart I see your temperature is a little higher than normal, but I'm going to give it to you straight." He sat in his chair and removed his gloves. "If it's what I think it is, you might have a sexually transmitted infection, but I won't know for sure until I run some tests."

"Wait!" I said hesitantly. I couldn't believe what I was hearing. My heart skipped a beat as my mind played catch up with what my ears had just heard.

"Let's not jump to conclusions. But I certainly don't want to rule it out either. I have been doing this for quite some time, which means I'm getting old. So I will run some tests to either back up what I assume or prove otherwise." he said with a reassuring smile.

"What type of tests?" I asked taking a deep breath.

"Well, what I am going to do is take a throat culture and we will perform a rapid test known as a DNA probe to determine what the virus is. From there we will administer treatment if need be. I don't want you to worry. It could just be a case of you coming down with the flu."

"So I could have a sexually transmitted disease?" I said closing my eyes and exhaling. I don't know if I really wanted to know the answer to that question. I wanted

271

to just disappear.

"Yes and no. It could be a number of things, Jason. Let's not assume anything, but I do need you to know that Gonorrhea and Chlamydia are on the rise in this city at an alarming rate. The good thing is if you are infected, both viruses are treatable. Meaning they can be knocked out with antibiotics. With early detection, we administer Ciprofloxacin or Cifixime for Gonorrhea, and Erythromycin to treat the Chlamydia. Now even if a patient does not show positive for Chlamydia, we administer that. A patient may have been exposed to it, but show no symptoms. So it's just a precautionary measure. And as I said before, this could just be a case of the Flu."

"Oh my God!" I said opening my eyes to look back at him.

"I understand how you might feel. I also want to do some blood work on you to see how everything else checks out, okay?

"Yes," I said. My tone was barely audible at that point. All I heard was sexually transmitted disease, throat cultures, and blood work. It felt as if I were about to become a damn science experiment.

"Do you have any questions for me?"

"Ummm...I'm just in shock." I said shaking my head.

"I can't think of anything right now. I just want to know what this is and go from there I guess?"

"Okay, well I have some questions for you then, okay?"

"Okay."

"When was your last HIV test?"

"Well maybe um...almost a year ago when I got my final physical from the military."

"What is the reason you haven't had one recently?"

"Well, I have had the same partner for some time now. And I assumed I had no reason to get one. I guess until recently." I paused and took a deep breath and looked down at my feet.

"Okay, well I have a few more questions for you, and then I will take a throat culture, an anal culture, and perform a blood draw to test for all other STI's and HIV infection, okay?"

"Okay, doc." I was thinking, did he just say anal culture? Oh my God. Now I have to have my booty swabbed with a Q-tip? This is not happening to me. I mean for a white guy, He was nice to look at, and I'd checked him out on my visits because he was eye candy. In my mind, I had a fantasy about us playing doctor and patient since he was gay, but this scenario was not part of that vision. I was so embarrassed, but he seemed to just be so carefree about this.

"Now the HIV results from the blood work will come in two weeks from today, but the cultures will be stat, so we will know today, okay? I can also do an oral swab for the HIV so we can try to rule that out."

"Alright."

"And since it's you, I will actually put a rush on the labs from the blood draw. I have a few connections I can utilize, okay?" He winked.

"Thank you. I appreciate that." I tried to smile, but it was a failed attempt from what I could tell.

He asked me a few more embarrassing questions and took the cultures along with the oral HIV swab. I asked my share of questions as well. Some I knew the answers to because I work in healthcare. He left the room and told me to try and maintain a positive attitude, informing me that he would return shortly with the results. Once again my thoughts were all over the place. I wanted desperately to punch Gary in the face for putting me through this stress. I lay back on the examining table.

Almost half an hour later Dr. Henderson walked back into the room with some paperwork in his hand. The hum of the ventilation system was starting to lull me to sleep. When I heard the door open, I quickly raised my body up from the table and studied his face as he sat down and put on his glasses. My heart was pounding. I was holding my breath and silently praying that he had some good news for me. He jotted down a few words on a post-it note and placed the folder down on his desk. He spun around slowly in his chair and faced me. I was a dry mouthed statue at that point. The world around me became so quiet, that I could hear the audible sound of my heartbeat in my ear. It was an unsettling silence. He removed his glasses and placed them in his lab coat pocket. He pursed his lips, clasped his hands together, and looked me directly in the eyes.

His mouth opened finally and the next thing I heard was as follows:

"Well, Jason... Upon looking at your lab results, I must tell you that unfortunately you tested positive..."